Now & Forever

Cynthia Dane

BARACHOU PRESS

Now & Forever

Published: 15th May 2018
Publisher: Barachou Press

Seven Years Ago
(Part 1)

James Merange dragged himself to the closest bar that was half-empty and still looked like it had a decent selection of bourbon. *Never thought of myself as a bourbon man, but today is totally a bourbon day.* Five hours. That's how long his meeting with his father's business associates had taken. Now that James was out of business school, he was expected to start carrying his weight in his family. That's what happened when he was born the only son to the traditional Meranges, let alone was the only *child.*

James was not a traditional kind of guy, however. But what else was he supposed to do with his life when he had no driving need to do something great? *Guy in my frat wanted to be an artist… so he became a pretty good artist. Fuck you, Feldman.* Why couldn't James have some talent? He had all this money to throw at it!

The bar was sophisticated, but none of the "top shelf" products on display screamed they were worth their weight in gold.

Good. That meant James could spare himself more networking and hobnobbing with the kind of *knobs* his father preferred. When he left the meeting twenty minutes ago, Albert was still going on about taking his business associates to a *lounge*. No, no, no. The only time James went to lounges was if his friends were going along. It was the only way to assure a half-decent time.

At least there wasn't a damn soul in the room, aside from the female bartender standing on the other side of the circular bar, cleaning glasses and facing the beer bottles on the shelf. James was so relieved to have an empty bar to himself that he courted serious fantasies of drinking his glass of bourbon and scrolling mindlessly on his iPhone. He had downloaded a new game that promised hours of mindless entertainment. Candy Crush. Yes, that was its name.

Yes, give me the booze, give me the NO BLASTED MUSIC ON SPEAKERS and give me bright colors and cartoon characters. It worked in Japan. About time America got with the program.

He had barely sat down when the female bartender rounded the corner and approached him with a smile.

The most gorgeous smile he had ever seen.

James knew he had been working too hard and too long when he swore he saw an angel descend from heaven and grace him with her presence. *Booze. Give me the booze now.* With any luck, James would soon be too drunk to give a shit that his brain, heart, and cock were telling him to marry the woman before him.

Years later, he would struggle to put into words what attracted him first about Gwenyth Mitchell, the only woman to knock him off his feet and *step on him* before he could get back up again. James had encountered his fair share of gorgeous women over the years. His undergrad years were nothing but a steady stream of pussy, most of those girls never standing a chance at *dating* him. Marriage? Yeah, right.

Yet why did he feel like he looked into the eyes of his future wife that night?

"What can I get you?" She spread her arms before him, fingers gripping her side of the mahogany-topped bar. "You look like you could use something strong. Long day at work?"

She asked the usual questions any good bartender looking for a tip relied on. But there was a tone to her voice that made her spunkier, more genuine than the common bartender fishing for tips. Had she felt it too? This instant connection that would end with her agreeing to go out with James? If he built up the guts to do it…

"Got any bourbon?" Amazing. His voice hadn't squeaked like he was a pubescent idiot.

"Bourbon? Oh, we got tons." She tossed errant strands of blond hair behind her ears. That loose bun wasn't going to get her far that night. Or was that the plan? Part of her flirtatious game? James was already losing this game, and he wasn't used to losing.

To anyone but the perfect opportunity, anyway.

"What brand's your poison?"

James asked for something dark and velvety. The bartender turned around to grab it, showing off her toned ass in the black jeans she wore like they were a second skin. James gawked at both cheeks as they flexed in denim. As long as he checked himself before she turned around again…

"What's your name?" he asked, before realizing that might have been the wrong thing to say. A woman like this? She was used to being flirted with every day.

"What's *your* name, stranger?" That smile was still the size of her golden aura when she turned around with a blessed bottle of booze. A glass popped onto the counter. "Haven't seen you around here before."

"James," was all he said. He didn't want to risk her recognizing his unique last name. Not in those parts.

"Better than Dylan or Ryder or whatever guys our age are named these days."

"It's a family name." James snorted to think of his great-grandfather, a man he had never met. "Ryder? Where the hell did you get that?"

"There were *two* of them in my bartending school alone. I think they were doing it on purpose."

James had his bourbon. He held it up and with a waggle of his eyebrows, offered his cheers to a friendly bartender.

"You still haven't told me your name," he said after taking a sip.

"Gwen."

"Wow."

"Wow?"

James almost blushed. He hadn't realized he said that out *loud.* "Haven't heard that name in a while. Is it so old it's new again?"

Gwen leaned against the bar with one hand, the other cocked on her hip. *If she poses like that anymore, I'm going to pop.* Maybe he should have more alcohol and go for the ol' whisky dick to prevent any embarrassing events in his pants.

"Go on," she said. "Guess what it's short for. I know you want to."

"Gwen…eth Paltrow?"

"Close." Gwen almost seemed impressed. "She spells it differently. I haven't met many girls who spell my name the way I do."

"Your choice or your parents'?"

She grinned. "Why can't I agree with them for once?"

A tap on the bar meant she had other things to take care of. James pulled out his phone, but couldn't bring himself to open the apps he wanted to play. He'd rather gaze longingly at Gwen, a vivacious woman who moved like she owned this bar. Maybe she did. Hell, James knew nothing about this joint. For all he knew, Gwen was a hospitality whizz who would one day own half the bars in town.

Almost made him feel like a pig to instantly wonder how she'd be in bed.

When he woke up that morning, he hadn't planned on trying to get laid. His brain was swarmed with business, family, and bullshit. That long-ass meeting more than guaranteed that he would go to bed early as soon as he got something to eat and took a shower. Now? He may be willing to make other plans, if the mood called for it.

Women like Gwen, though? They weren't easy. Usually. Not that James would want her to be. Couldn't half the fun be the seduction?

"How long have you been working here?" he called after her.

Gwen glanced at him over her shoulder. A mini-fridge door closed. Lemon slices were put away. "Long enough to know that you're not a regular here, and have no reason to be asking me that other than to flirt."

"Am I that transparent?"

She stood in the circular groove of the bar. "Kind of. But you're cute, so I'll let it slide."

"Knew it. You ladies already let us cute ones get away with everything."

"Just don't let it go to your head. I don't want to have to call the bouncer to deal with you."

"Who's the bouncer?"

Gwen cocked her head, a mischievous grin that only someone like James could appreciate catching his attention once more. "Me."

"No way."

"Care to find out?"

"No way."

Laughing, Gwen asked him how his drink was and insisted that she had other things to do.

That's how it went for the next few weeks, when James came up with any excuse to swing by that bar and see his favorite bartender. He never asked Gwen out, because he was afraid of ruining what they tentatively had: friendly banter and friendlier conversation. The fact she always wore tight pants and tight shirts made the visits extra special. James appreciated some fodder to take home to his imagination.

He often wondered if she looked forward to his visits – and if she wanted him as much as he wanted her.

CHAPTER 1

GWEN

There wasn't enough wine in the world to get Gwen through this dinner.

She was on her second glass already, and it was only the first course of Albert Merange's birthday dinner. *So many better ways to spend a Sunday night.* Sunday nights were Gwen's favorite times to put on her pajamas and stare at the TV until bedtime. Preferably while in the arms of her partner, James. Not that they had indulged in much cuddling in the past year.

Gwen stared at the bottom of her empty wineglass while a servant took away the bits of her salad she would rather not put into her mouth. *Suppose I should hold off on drinking more until I've had something more substantial to eat.* She looked up and met Albert's eyes from the end of the dining table. He quickly looked away. Gwen wanted more wine. Or a cocktail, preferably. Maybe some straight vodka.

James's father always maintained a tenuous respect for the woman who might be his daughter-in-law, but Gwen had often suspected that he tolerated her because he thought her a flash-in-the-pan love affair that might last three years at most. James and Gwen had been in their early twenties when they first got together. The Meranges had told their only child that he could sow all the wild oats he wanted – as long as he sterilized those oats, first.

But Gwen hadn't been a temporary girlfriend. She graduated to James's domestic partner and was now as synonymous with his name as he was with hers. Over seven years, Gwen Mitchell had integrated herself into her boyfriend's high-society life. She had heiresses for friends. Memberships at invitation-only clubs. (Perhaps not all of them, but the ones she had been invited to were satisfactory enough for her commoner background.) A contract that said, should she and James break up, she would receive whatever she required to start her life over again elsewhere. Many out-of-towners were shocked to find out that Gwen wasn't an heiress. Blending in with the lot of neurotic, spoiled assholes had been easy enough.

One of her closest friends was Charlotte Williams, one such heiress who had been the first to take Gwen by the hand and show her how to make the most of her station if she insisted on falling in love with a multimillionaire (in his own right) like James Merange. Charlotte, whose family was close friends with the Meranges, had come to tonight's birthday dinner at Gwen's request. *I don't want to be alone with these people.* Bad enough Gwen had to sit next to James's mother. At least she could see Charlotte across from her, helping her ailing father with his uncut potatoes as the main course came out for them to enjoy.

"Is this goose?" Mr. Williams asked the birthday boy. "How did you manage to snag some at this time of year?"

"You know I have my connections." Albert accepted his second glass of wine as the sommelier made the rounds of the table. Gwen exhibited great decorum when she turned down a third glass and instead sucked on her ice water. *Dessert. I will have a third glass at dessert.* She would really need it if the birthday dessert was Albert's favorite cherry pie. Blech.

Mrs. Ophelia Merange had her wineglass topped up before leaning in toward the Williamses. "My husband humbles himself on his birthday, you see. He managed to catch not one, but *two* geese last hunting season. Really was a magnificent bit of skill, wasn't it, darling?"

Albert did not blush, but he propped himself up in his seat and said, "Skill and luck often go hand-in-hand. We had the first goose for Christmas, and the second for tonight. Hopefully, my grandson will be old enough this year to enjoy it for the first time. A love for well-roasted fowl is built into our bloodline." He turned to his son, sitting between himself and Gwen. "Isn't it, James?"

He, like his girlfriend Gwen, had been quiet for most of the dinner. But when his own father asked him a question, he couldn't simply sit in silence. Even when one of those words had made a shudder go down both his and Gwen's spines.

"Don't have much of a taste for duck anymore," he attempted to say with humor. "But I do love a good turkey."

The goose had been carved in the kitchen, unlike the mess back at Christmas when Albert insisted on cutting open the bird at the table in front of everyone, including his infant grandson. Patrick had wailed to see the golden goose split open like one of his stuffed toys. His mother had ushered him out of the room and didn't come back to eat until the child had been put down for a nap.

"You should see the boy," Albert continued, speaking to his friend Mr. Williams. "Still a bit on the small side, but so was his father when he was his age." He reached into his pocket and pulled out his phone. "I remember telling his mother that we would have to find him a wet nurse to make sure he was good and fed."

"Albert, dear…" Mrs. Ophelia Merange held in her exasperation with considerable taste. "Mr. Williams and his daughter don't want to hear about that."

"Look! Right here!" Albert showed a picture on his phone to his friend. "Have you ever seen such an adorable little boy? Gives me hope that the best of our genes are really plowing through the generations."

Mr. Williams adjusted his glasses. Charlotte politely poked at her dinner. Mrs. Merange studied her son's face, gauging his reaction.

James and Gwen both reached for their wineglasses. James drank the rest of his while Gwen was sorely reminded that she hadn't opted for the refill.

"Oh, my…" Mr. Williams looked across the table, to James, a grin touching his wrinkled cheeks. "He really does have your nose. Isn't that remarkable?"

James forced a smile of acknowledgment. "I suppose so."

He took Gwen's hand beneath the table. She placed her napkin next to her plate of goose and potatoes and excused herself to the bathroom.

That was what she had dreaded the most when she agreed to come to Albert's birthday dinner. The man was *so* smitten with his grandson, that he couldn't help but shove the boy in everyone's faces. Especially Gwen's.

Because he's not my son. He belonged to some other woman, a bastard sanctioned by the Merange's and their friends, the Welshes.

Gwen would never forget that horrifying night one year ago, at a gala before Christmas, when Cassandra Welsh waltzed into town with a baby on her hip. The whisper in high society was that one of her many, *many* lovers was the father, and the reason she skipped down wasn't because of a mental meltdown, but because she was pregnant with a bastard baby. James, the man who once called Cassandra his best childhood friend, had been his usual mix of concerned for her well-being and utterly delighted by the shitstorm brewing in town. There was no one more invested in gossip and "hot messes" than James Merange.

Until this one bit him in the ass.

The baby was his. Even a DNA test proved that. That night – that long ago, far away night that almost ruined their lives – Gwen ran the gamut of emotions that went from *The Bastard Cheated on Me* to *The Welshes Did WHAT?*

James had not, in fact, cheated on his partner of seven years. Instead, semen that he had preemptively stored in a bank upon reaching adulthood had been pilfered by the Welshes, because they were desperate for an heir, and Cassandra would only settle for having James's baby. The worst part? James was never allowed any say in it. His father had signed off on the release of the genetic material for Cassandra to use in a sterile doctor's office. Apparently, it had worked.

How could Gwen be angry at the man she loved for something beyond his control? How was he supposed to know that his parents still carried certain powers he never anticipated? And how could he face his sudden fatherhood alone? Gwen couldn't leave him. Not when he was innocent. Not when they still loved each other.

Still, such events that not even the likes of James could have ever foreseen, put unprecedented strains on their relationship.

Before that night, we were as happy as ever. After that night, they had drifted apart, until Gwen often wondered how much more she could take before she opted for the stipend and moving to the west coast. Alone.

Albert was one of her least favorite people. *He* was the one who conspired with the Welshes to get the grandson he didn't think he would otherwise have, since Gwen wasn't good enough, and she and James had often discussed the idea of never having children. Something he probably ran by his father a time or two, considering the family was already small and had amassed quite the fortune over the generations.

That man was the family type. Not that he was ever so involved, James made sure to explain, but he loved the idea of children and probably thought of them as proof of his virility. "*Must've sent him mad to know his wife could only have one.*" Like it had driven him mad when he realized he and his real love, Sarah Welsh, would never be together as anything more than an illicit affair that transcended decades. *James's mother is more humiliated than I am on a daily basis.*

This family was so fucked.

After the awkward dinner concluded and presents were exchanged over cherry pie, James insisted that he had an early meeting Monday morning and needed to get home. Albert asked his son to stay at the family estate and leave early in the morning, but the matter had already been decided once Gwen impatiently waited in the passenger seat of James's latest vehicular acquisition, a 2018 Jaguar coupe. She popped some gum into her mouth and willed the car to get them home as quickly as possible. The only thing worse than awkward dinners like that were the awkward silences that always ensued on the drives home.

"God," James muttered as they pulled out of the estate's driveway, "I hope I didn't have too much wine."

"I didn't have enough."

That was all they said during the twenty-five-minute drive home.

For the past five years, they had made their primary residence a two-story colonial manor (James swore it would've been a proper manor in the 18th century, but now it was simply charming) in a gated community that boasted as many expendable heirs as it did self-made millionaires. Having a proper house suited them more than living in a penthouse or expansive apartment downtown. Besides, the community was only a ten-minute drive from the city center, and that accounted for mild traffic. All the amenities without the hectic pace of city life.

James hid in his man cave – *Sorry, his office* – while Gwen took a long, hot shower and kicked her heels up in front of the TV with a bottle of hard cider in her hand. Their one live-in servant, Rebecca, asked the lady of the house if she required any other refreshments before turning in for the night. Gwen asked her what the hell she was doing asking that on the staffs' day off. Deferential until the end, Rebecca retreated to her private quarters on the other side of the house.

"Did you know," Gwen asked John Oliver on HBO, "that Rebecca came *highly* recommended by James's parents when we were in the market for a new maid?" She wanted to gag. While Rebecca was more than qualified to take care of a vintage house while the owners kept to their deliriously busy schedules, she was also a trained doula and nanny. The hint hadn't been bigger if Albert Merange rented a billboard to tell Gwen to get knocked up if she insisted on infiltrating the family.

James stumbled into the shower without a word to his partner. Gwen finished her cider and crawled into bed, hoping that the alcohol would make her eyelids heavy.

The bed sank with James's added weight a few minutes later. For a brief, hypnotic second, Gwen was pulled in by the scent of his shampoo and the sandalwood soap he used on the rest of his body. That's what happened when she was half-asleep and presented with the comforts of their past – she forgot everything that had happened and happily slung her arm across her partner's chest.

He held her hand in his, chest slowly rising and falling with his breaths. Gwen would have forgotten what she was always so angry about if it weren't for him opening his mouth.

"What are you doing tomorrow?"

She slowly opened her eyes to the darkness of their bedroom. "I'm going to brunch with one of the fundraising committees I'm on. Then I guess I'm going to the gym. Why? What are you doing after your morning meetings?"

His silence spoke a thousand words.

"To the Welshes?"

"Yeah."

Gwen turned over without a word. She loved James, and loved that he was willing to be a father to a boy he never knew existed until a year ago, but the amount of time he spent at Welsh Grove visiting his son made her nervous. Not the part about the boy.

The part about everyone else in that family, constantly conspiring to marry him to a woman he claimed to have never loved – like *that.*

CHAPTER 2

JAMES

James parked in his usual spot in front of the main Welsh house. A servant always grabbed his keys and parked the car elsewhere, but James had no idea where his vehicles disappeared. For all he knew, someone was paid to rife through his belongings, looking for proof that he was… something. He hadn't figured out that part of the conspiracy.

The head butler awaited him at the front door. The man nodded his head without a smile as James fixed the buttons on his jacket and entered Welsh Grove, the expansive country estate that had been in the family since before America was a country. *This house is older than mine.* And bigger. Much, much bigger.

James always followed the butler to one of three rooms: the upstairs nursery, the downstairs playroom or, if he had been a bad boy recently, the salon where either Cassandra or her mother Madam Sarah Walsh awaited. The last time he was shown to the salon, Madam Welsh was quite upset that the father of her grandson had *opinions* on where Patrick should go to school.

Thankfully, on that otherwise nondescript Monday, James was shown into the downstairs playroom where his son sat with Irene the nanny, flipping through large picture books and smashing blocks together.

My son. He never got used to thinking that, even though Patrick Merange's face was unmistakably like his father's. James wasn't there when his son was born. Nor was he aware of his existence until Cassandra thought it prudent to inform him that, "*Oh, yes, by the way, I had your baby. Turns out you don't need intercourse for that to happen these days.*" The first time James met his son was after the bomb had been dropped on his life. Shocked. Scared. Appalled that this had happened without his knowledge. He knew plenty of men who had children they never knew about, but could it really shock them if they had done the deed with the woman? James and Cassandra had never been involved like *that.* He hadn't been with anyone but Gwen since they met seven years ago. *I partied it up in college, but I think I would know about illegitimate children by now. Maybe. Perhaps.* James was made of money. Those women would've come after his child support within two weeks of giving birth.

Cassandra hadn't wanted his money, though. She had plenty of her own with her family, and Grandpa Merange was more than generous with the presents and trust funds already set up for his grandson's future. Honestly, if James had wanted *out* of this situation, he was more than free to sign away any of his parental rights and go about his life. But he wasn't like that. Once the fog cleared and he realized *I have a son,* all he could think about was being anything but a deadbeat dad.

That didn't make these weekly, sometimes twice or thrice weekly, meetings any easier.

"Look, Patrick," Irene said, bending down from her chair and looking the boy in the blue eyes, "your daddy's here."

Patrick turned with excitement. "Pa!" he cried, holding up a block with the letter *J* on it. Close enough.

"There's my boy." James knelt beside his son and beckoned for one of the blocks. There hadn't been enough time to go home after his meeting to change into something more comfortable than the three-piece suit he wore for work. Perfect for Patrick, who was more entranced by neckties than anything else on James's person. "Are you being good for Irene?"

The forty-something nanny smiled to say, "He's an absolute angel after he's had his nap. Aren't you, Patrick?"

Patrick fell onto his back with a mighty *plop* even his father could appreciate.

"Like I said," James said with a chuckle, "that's my boy right there."

Irene laughed, going into an attached room. The boys needed some bonding time – alone.

"So…" James sat next to his quiet son. "Got a girlfriend yet?"

Patrick stuck his finger in his nose and conducted a treasure hunt for the ages.

"It's fine. Someone around here will teach you how to do that in private. Handkerchiefs, boy. The wave of the future."

James didn't dread spending time with his son. He always assumed he would be a perfectly fine father, should that day come, and he liked children well enough. *I didn't think it would happen so soon. I'm barely thirty.* If it did happen by now, he would've had plenty of warning. Time to get used to the idea of being a father.

Opportunity to get his affairs in order.

Not to mention… Gwenny would be the mother, right? That was the crux of this situation. Not only had James been bamboozled by his own family, but poor Patrick had been robbed of a proper one. He may have been given James's last name, but he lived with and was raised by the Welshes. He was *their* heir. That had been made clear when the dust settled, anger subsided, and everyone had a *lovely* sit down to talk about Patrick. The Welshes wanted the boy as a guarantee of their longevity. James was more than welcomed to make Patrick his heir – in fact, it was encouraged – but the Welshes expressed that they would not be affronted if James had other children and prioritized them in his line of succession. "*After all,*" Sarah Welsh had said with one of her haughty sighs, "*the poor little dear is a bastard. We don't expect you to do anything.*"

Difficult to think about those things when staring into the big eyes of a baby boy. Patrick grinned at his father, who matched the smile before picking him up.

For an hour, James distracted himself with the delight that was his son, because he couldn't ruminate on the injustices of their families when an innocent child was in his arms. He didn't worry about the boy's future. He didn't wonder what would happen when he died, and Patrick thought, "*Where's my money, Daddy?*" Nor did he spend his time thinking about Gwen.

He thought about Gwen before and after playtime, though. She was all he could think about anymore.

Gwen had only met Patrick once. That night, over a year ago, when Cassandra confessed what she had done and implored them to meet her son. *Their* son.

That meeting had been brief. While James stayed behind to behold what his genetics could create, Gwen showed herself out.

They had never been the same since.

"What do you think?" James asked, showing his son pictures on his phone. "Beautiful, ain't she? That's the woman your old man thinks is the greatest in the world."

Patrick was more interested in what the buttons on James's phone could do than what the picture of Gwen looked like. *This was taken one month before that fateful night.* They had spent Thanksgiving in Bermuda, soaking up the sun and lounging around on pristine beaches. It was the last time they truly had no cares in the world. It was also the last time Gwen was full of the usual life James had come to love over the years.

Of course, James worried about her. How could he not? She was his partner! She may not yet be mother of his children, but she was as good as his wife after seven years, and he cared enough to note the difference whenever his parents harangued him for still being unmarried in his thirties.

Soon, Patrick would be old enough to understand that his parents were not married, and that his father had another woman he lived with. Would they get along? Would Gwen *want* Patrick in their colonial manor as he grew up, even if it were just on the weekends? They knew how to keep their bedroom business private around a child, but the Welshes probably would not be impressed to know that the father of their heir liked his kinky games. It was one of the things that had attracted Gwen!

There are other things they won't like about my personal life. No, it had nothing to do with James's reputation as a heartful prankster, although he hadn't indulged in any games for two years. It had everything to do with the whispers that he might be too queer to be around a growing young gentleman of the American peerage.

I need this boy to grow up with me, otherwise the Welshes will turn him into another shell of parroted opinions and harmful anecdotes. That was less acceptable these days, especially when the common man became wiser to the ways of the rich and closed-off. The last thing James needed was another young man growing up without the ability to think for himself, espouse empathy, and get along with people outside of his group. James had known that would be his realm of parenting the moment he saw the way Sarah Welsh bundled Patrick up and sing one of the most racist nursery rhymes James had heard in decades. Naturally, Madam Welsh didn't understand the problem.

She also didn't understand that James would prefer to have a whole *hour* with his son.

"There you are." That clipped and snooty tone summoned James from the floor, where he sat with Patrick and built blocks into colorful towers. Sarah Welsh sauntered into the playroom, uncharacteristically dressed in trousers and a long-sleeved blouse that left the top button undone. Her recently coifed hair was more reminiscent of modern Dame Helen Mirren than a traditional Jayne Mansfield style that Sarah so usually loved. *It's the grandmother look, isn't it?* No offense to Ms. Mirren, of course. James merely assumed this meant that Sarah Welsh was updating her look to match that of a young gentleman's sporty grandmother.

He always greatly disliked this woman. He greatly disliked her even more when he discovered the ongoing affair between her and his father, a discovery made when James was in college and realizing that his parents weren't the infallible gods of morality. That was solidified last year when he realized his father was the one who conspired with Madam Welsh to get the grandchild of their dreams, since James refused to be attracted to his childhood friend Cassandra in the way *they* preferred. In their day, a betrothal would have sealed James's fate, and that would've been it.

But this wasn't their day anymore.

"Such a lovely Monday, isn't it?" James asked. He stood, carefully shadowing his son while the vulture circled.

"Absolutely gorgeous," Madam Welsh said without a smile. "Care to enjoy it with me? We have something to discuss."

"Five more minutes with Patrick, please."

Sarah said nothing as she patted her grandson on the head and showed herself out of the playroom. That suited James fine. He might even take *ten* more minutes with his son, Sarah's wishes be damned. Quality time with a boy he sometimes only saw once a week was worth more than an audience with a woman he could hardly stand to look at.

Irene re-entered the playroom in time for Patrick's nap. Perfect timing, since the boy was falling asleep in James's arms and occasionally kicking up a fuss because he wanted his favorite stuffed toy and blanket. James reluctantly passed him to the nanny, who absconded with him upstairs to his nursery. James remained in the hallway until he could no longer see the head of his son's dark head.

To the salon he must go.

Sarah Welsh awaited him at her usual table by the window, where the sunshine was strongest on summer days and visitors enjoyed a view of the gardens Madam Welsh had overseen for the forty years she had lived in Welsh Grove. It was also conveniently close to the main kitchen, which allowed a collection of tea and cookies she couldn't help but consume every time she sat down in the salon, guests or no.

"Tea, James?"

He sat across from her. "No, thank you."

"You must try my new chef's no bake cookies. To die for."

"I'd rather get right to what you wanted to talk about."

Sarah snorted. "In a hurry, James?"

Yes. To get away from you. There were many reasons to thank his lucky stars for never falling in love with Cassandra, and never having to deal with this woman as his mother-in-law was one of them. Gwen's parents were absolute delights compared to the

Welshes, and they had the education and conversational properties of ten-year-olds.

"I have obligations later this afternoon."

"Very well." Sarah took a sip of her tea before saying, "It's about your relationship with Ms. Mitchell."

The corners of James's mouth already twitched. "Dare I ask what you've heard this time? Why you think it's any of your business?"

"It became my business once you decided to involve yourself with Patrick's upbringing."

"The boy's already a bastard." One of the worst things a poor boy could be, according to the society James grew up in – and often escaped. "What I do hardly correlates to how he'll be treated beyond that." Besides, it was the twenty-first century, and America. Nobody cared about *bastards* anymore.

"He is already at a disadvantage, yes. Which is why I am invested in making his transition into society the easiest possible. The last thing I want for my grandson is for him to be surrounded by rumors from his father's camp."

"You're best buds with my father. What else could you ask for?"

"Your compliance when it comes to your love life."

James could no longer hide the frown crowning his complexion. "Come out and say that you find Gwenyth distasteful."

"What I think of *that* is beyond my prerogative. You've already asserted that you see her as a life-partner. That, James, is not what I am worried about."

"Then what? Worried that she would not make an appropriate stepmother for your grandson?"

"I wouldn't know. She's never come to visit him."

"Is that the issue, then?"

"Would you please let me finish?" Sarah checked her exasperation. *Can't be too unladylike, even in front of me.* "I'm worried about the rumors swarming about you two like busy little bees. Don't suppose you've noticed, but there are many whispers that you two are facing a difficult time in your relationship."

"That is our business."

"So you do not refute it?"

James leaned in across the table. "Rather hard to maintain tranquility in one's relationship when bombs are dropped upon you like it's London in the '40s."

"I suppose that makes us the Nazis."

I mean, in a way… Did eugenics play a part in the creation of Patrick Merange? "Gwen has been taking the news of my sudden parentage rather hard. It can't be that shocking that she's having trouble adjusting. The woman had her trust in me completely shaken. For five minutes, she thought I had an affair behind her back. As a woman, I'm sure you can understand…" He stopped, laughing. For a few minutes, *he* had forgotten that Sarah Welsh knew all about extramarital affairs!

"Is something funny, James?"

"You mean besides this whole situation?"

"I think you would want to do the right thing for the boy you think so highly of."

"He's definitely a little squirt."

"Yes. Quite." Sarah sipped more of her tea, thoughts formulating behind her bright hazel eyes. "Let me cut to the chase, James."

"Finally."

"I think it would be in Patrick's best interest if you and Ms. Mitchell finally parted ways. Clearly, it is no longer a healthy relationship, and my grandson deserves to be surrounded by only the…"

James interrupted with what she *really* meant. "I suppose if I break up with Gwen, then I have the perfect opportunity to be with the mother of my child, yes?"

"I didn't say that."

"You thought it."

"What mother doesn't want her daughter to be happy?"

James stood up. "Trust me, Madam, I will take your suggestion to heart. Now, if it's all right with you, I have that obligation to attend."

He had to leave before his anger got the best of him. The most painful thing? Knowing his son was locked away in his nursery, and he wouldn't see him again for a few days.

Yet he could go home to Gwen. That was his primary obligation.

CHAPTER 3

GWEN

The day was clear and beautiful for mid-winter, but Gwen couldn't bring herself to enjoy it. Not even when she popped out of her taxi and inhaled the fresh air blowing in from a community garden on the other side of the street. She cinched her winter coat closer to her body and entered the unmarked building closely guarded by security personnel posing as uniformed doormen.

Everything about this building, from its high-security, to its rooftop clubs and restaurants, had been unknown to Gwen before she met James. Back then, she was a bartender scraping by with roommates and nothing but a GED in her back pocket. She passed this building every day, assuming it was offices for lawyers and rent-controlled apartments. Without a fancy name slapped on the side or ornate architecture to attract the eye, she never had a reason to believe some of the city's richest and most influential either lived in this building or conducted their social lives within its confines.

Gwen had been here innumerable times over the past seven years. Now, she didn't think twice about saying hello to security and nodding her head to the well-dressed receptionist rising from his high-tech desk with a practiced smile they still taught at finishing schools around the city. She relayed the name of the café she had reservations at and was permitted into the guarded elevator on the other side of the lobby. The elevator attendant tipped his hat and pressed a polite finger against the number for the top floor.

It didn't take me long to get used to this, did it? The café was members only, but Gwen had been invited within two years of publicly dating James. That was two years of proving herself as a well-mannered lady – and a good-time friend to the heiresses who found her refreshing and charming. Some women, like Jasmine Cole, struggled to fit in with the raucous group that ran the city from behind the scenes, but Gwen was a natural when it came to socializing and buttering people up. How else did she get good enough at bartending to work at a place James would soon frequent after college? The man didn't mind getting down and dirty with commoners, but he didn't exactly hang out at Pat's Pizzeria and Tavern on Friday nights.

It also helped that James's closest friends tended to be more easygoing heirs and businessmen who didn't care about Gwen's pedigree as long as she could take a joke and dish them back. Which was why it was only natural that she would become somewhat close with heiress Kathryn Alison, the girlfriend of James's best friend, Ian Mathers.

Kathryn rose from their table as soon as she saw Gwen emerge from the elevator and pass the maître d's podium. They exchanged kisses to the cheeks and sat down in time for the waiter to approach. Gwen knew exactly what she wanted before she sat down.

"I hear the oysters are to die for this season." Kathryn handed the one-page menu back to the waiter before refocusing her attention on Gwen. "And the goose, but I'm trying to cut back on my meat consumption. Again."

She said that with a sigh. Gwen couldn't help but reply, "I had plenty of goose to last me a lifetime yesterday at Albert's birthday dinner."

"Oh, yikes."

"Tell me about it. If Charlotte and her father hadn't come to hog some of the conversation, I might've jumped out the window."

"How is she these days? I haven't seen her in ages."

"Who, Charlotte?" Gwen shrugged. "She was hopping around Europe for most of twenty-seventeen. Don't think she got back until last month. You could tell, too. She's so jetlagged."

"Jetlagged and boozed up is probably the only way to get through Albert Merange's birthday dinner."

Gwen almost choked on her ice water. "You have *nooo* idea."

"Go on. What is that bastard doing to ruin your life now?"

Nobody was more in-the-know on the drama than Kathryn and Ian, who were not only close to Gwen and James, but doubtlessly spent hours gossiping about the knowledge they had and the general, socially elite public didn't. Everyone by now knew that something shady had gone down to create Patrick Merange – although there were many who refused to believe that James hadn't cheated and Gwen needed to pack her bags – but only those closest to the family knew exactly what had transpired to irreparably damage familial bonds.

"Jesus." Kathryn held up her cocktail and shook her head. "That man has got to be one of the biggest narcissists around, and that says so much. No wonder he and Sarah Welsh were meant to be together. She's the second biggest narcissist in town."

Gwen let out an unladylike laugh that made her the target of everyone else's glares. *Piss off, princesses.* Most of the lunch crowd was made up of matriarchs and their heiress daughters. If someone wasn't drunk right now, they could still be called a functioning alcoholic outside of the café. *Some are better at hiding it than others.* There was a reason the menu there was so short – most of the patrons drank their lunches.

Gwen didn't give a fuck if some half-high heiress found her uncouth. Nor did she care if some businessman's trophy wife stuck up her nose at Gwen's presence. Most of them didn't have any room to talk. Gwen knew how to blend in. Sometimes, though, she didn't give a shit!

"How are you and James doing?"

Questions like that were what made half the women in the room functioning alcoholics. Gwen certainly wished she had ordered something stronger than iced tea.

"We're not *doing* anything." Sighing, Gwen sat back in her seat, legs properly crossed and handkerchief laying across her lap.

"Still? Damn. Thought that maybe after a year…"

"When your trust in someone is that damaged, it's difficult to recover."

"Even when you find out the truth so quickly?"

"It's not only about James…" Gwen didn't know how to explain it. Any anger she felt toward James didn't have to do with *him,* per se. He was innocent in this, and many women would say it was admirable that he was so adamant about being a father to a boy. "It's his family. I don't trust them."

"Ahh, yes. The Meranges are… ruthless."

"I know, but they're not as ruthless as the Welshes, and I'm mixed up with them, too."

"Have you guys gone to couple's therapy yet?"

"We've tried." Gwen didn't want to think about that. "Didn't really get anywhere."

Kathryn didn't say anything, much to Gwen's relief. So when she opened her mouth to ask another question, Gwen was compelled to interrupt with the crux of her problem.

"I keep thinking that I should cut my losses and leave."

The silence now simmering at their table was much alike the silences in couple's therapy. *I feel terrible saying that, but it's the truth. Who else can I tell right now?* She had already dropped hints to her friend Charlotte that she was thinking of breaking up with James for good. It didn't matter how much a woman loved a man. It also sometimes didn't matter if that man had a good heart and had never hurt her in the seven years they had been together. Sometimes, the powers that be – the ones really pulling the puppet strings in the background – were dark enough that a girl needed to know when to run.

"Leave, huh?" Kathryn's hands remained wrapped around her cocktail. "I can't even imagine it. You and James have been together for as long as I can remember."

"Yeah, well…" Gwen sipped her cold tea. *Not enough lemon.* Nobody gave her enough lemon slices, even if she asked for two. "Things change. We had a good run, but it's kinda like a TV show, you know? At some point, everything jumps the shark, and it feels like the writers are putting in outrageous, contrived scenarios to get more ratings. That's what this whole past year has felt like. While everyone around us is hooking up and getting married, we're over here falling apart."

Kathryn cocked her head. Usually, she wore it up in a tight, blond coil that made people ask if it hurt. Today, however, she wore it down and to one side. Luscious, silky locks that were the envy of every brunette heiress in New England. *My hair isn't really blond. I wonder how many people know that?* James knew it. Charlotte knew it. Gwen had been dying her light brown hair blond for so many years that not even Amber Mayview, queen of fake blond hair, could hold a candle to Gwen's layering and highlighting skills.

It ruined the texture of her hair.

"Is it really about the baby, though? And the in-laws?"

Gwen didn't dare make eye contact with Kathryn as she considered that. "There have always been issues to the undercurrent of our relationship. No relationship is perfect, you know."

"Don't I. Being with Ian isn't a walk in the park, no matter how long you're with him."

"I can imagine." Gwen drummed her fingers against the table. "I love James. Before we were blindsided with a baby, we had issues, but we could deal with them. We were working through them. I can't deal with those issues *and* this bullshit. It's bad enough the whole world knows about what the Welshes did. Now I'm a stepmom? Just like that? It's way too much. James and I still aren't even sure where we're going over the long term. It would've been one thing if I got knocked up. Or if he at least had *slept* with the mother of his child…"

Kathryn couldn't stand the silence, could she? "That's the danger we sign up for committing to men who have… uh, pasts."

Right. Because Kathryn was the one woman who understood what kind of "past" James had. *Ian is probably worse.* Gwen had heard all the stories about their frat boy days. "*Endless pussy for days, Gwenny. I'm not ashamed to admit your boy here took part in the plunder. Only with the willing, of course. But, you know me… lots of women willing…*" He always told those stories with a wink and the kind of charming smile that made it a hilarious anecdote as opposed to, "*How many illegitimate children do you have, James?*"

Kathryn was not the mothering kind, like Gwen. For Kathryn, she probably worried every day she would have stepmother-hood dropped on her the day one of Ian's ex-lovers appeared with a kid that looked like him. Well, it had happened to Gwen, but it was all wrong!

"Don't mind me," Gwen said. "Musing out loud."

"You have every right to be…"

Gwen cut her friend off with a gasp. As if God had decided to fuck with her some more, the elevator doors to the members-only café opened to admit a contingency of Welsh women.

No, not the ones from Wales. (Although the Welshes certainly claimed to be… Welsh.) The ones that had set out to destroy Gwen's life and relationship.

Madam Sarah Walsh walked in first, her trendy trousers sashaying with her legs as she corralled a toy poodle on a leash. Behind her?

Her only child. Cassandra.

Gwen hadn't seen the oft talked-about woman in months. Seen her pictures? Yes. Heard the outrageous stories? Obviously. Seen her in the flesh, let alone heard that whispery voice that *somehow* seduced half the men in the world but couldn't make James Merange bend enough to bed her?

No. Gwen had made sure of that. Yet she supposed she couldn't completely avoid a wealthy heiress around those parts.

"Wow." Kathryn drank the last of her cocktail. "*Wow.*"

Gwen couldn't take her eyes off the woman who had effectively ruined her life. Cassandra Welsh was one of *those* effortless beauties who managed to be both wounded deer and strong, independent woman. Gwen had it on good authority – such as Kathryn's – that Cassandra was a master seductress who could change her appearance like a manipulative chameleon. That's how she was able to bed men who preferred their women loud and proud, and men who saw themselves as the hero in every girlfriend's story. *She's got problems. I can't hold that against her.* The truly terrible thing about all this coming out in public discussion was how much of Cassandra's mental health had been put on trial. Then again, Gwen often mused, no woman went around acting like that without having some sort of issue. Apparently, Cassandra's was a perpetually broken heart.

Not my fault she can't seduce James! Gwen had to control her breathing before it fled her body and left her a withered shell.

"What are the odds?" Kathryn asked.

"Pretty good, apparently." Gwen grabbed her things before the waiter brought her lunch. "I'm sorry, Kathryn. I can't…"

"I understand." She put her hand on Gwen's. "I'll take care of the bill and have your meal forwarded to your house."

"Thanks." Even after seven years, Gwen forgot that was a service the rich relied on, like poor people asking for Styrofoam boxes at the end of a meal. "I'll make it up to you later this week. Maybe at the gym?"

"Sounds great."

Gwen intended to leave with dignity. She wouldn't spare the Welshes a single glance, nor would she try to hide her identity on her way out the door. *I don't care if they never see me. I don't care if they* do *see me and are scandalized by my beating heart.* Gwen cared if they thought her a coward, instead of a woman making a harsh statement.

Haughty heiresses and their hoity-toity mothers played these games every single day. How many women had scoffed and left a room when Gwen first started coming to these places? Everyone had their petty, *petty* lines they drew in the metaphorical sand when someone they found displeasing walked into a room.

Gwen had never indulged in that socialite's right until Cassandra Fucking Welsh.

"*Where's your son?*" Gwen wanted to ask her. "*Is he with a nanny right now, when he could be with his father? How much do you really care about the man you claim to love?*"

Much to Gwen's chagrin, however, she caught Sarah Welsh's eye.

"Ms. Mitchell!" she called with that bird-like voice she loved to unleash upon Gwen. "How are you?"

Gwen stopped in her tracks. Half the café put down their utensils and stared at them, ready for the show of the week.

Gwen slowly turned her head, sharp, narrowing eyes glaring at the mastermind behind Operation Baby. *You're the real person I despise in all of this, Welsh.* You're *the one who put the diabolical idea in your daughter's head.*

Cassandra wouldn't spare Gwen a glance. Perhaps it wasn't because she thought herself so much better than Gwen. If anything, it was probably because she felt at least a little shame for what she had done, which was more shame than Sarah would ever feel.

Narcissists. They flocked together, didn't they?

"Doing quite well, thank you, Madam Welsh." Gwen spared her only the slightest smile. More like a smirk than a movement of mirth. "I trust that things are going your way, as usual?"

Sarah threw that smirk right back at her. "Why wouldn't it be, Ms. Mitchell?"

Gwen was close enough that she didn't hesitate to flip them a bird on her way out the door. *Talk about that for a few weeks, you fucking hags.* Not classy, but sometimes she had to put her low-class rearing to work. Anything good enough for a bar was good enough for this prissy café.

CHAPTER 4

JAMES

He lay in bed, yawning and attempting to fall asleep before the *Friends* rerun ended on TV. The shower in the master bathroom continued to lull him into a doze, but he couldn't sleep. Not with so much always on his mind.

James had heard a rumor on the grapevine that his lovely Gwenny had flipped off the Welshes after running into them at lunch. *That's my girl.* It was that kind of spunk that attracted him to her. A drop-dead gorgeous woman with a mouth like fire and heels that weren't afraid to castrate a man who got in her way? Clearly, Gwen Mitchell had no idea what she was getting into when she agreed to go home with James one late night in their early twenties.

Still, it was going to be a "thing," wasn't it? The only reason James heard about it was because one of his old frat buddies wanted to *warn* him that the grapevine was giving people whiplash after that display. If a man had come up to him to whisper in his ear that Gwen had caused a minor scene, then it was going to be big. Eventually.

Not that James really cared. Gwen had simply done what he hadn't been able to get away with recently.

Not gonna lie, it turns me on. Like the thought of Gwen naked in the shower right now turned him on. Damn. How long had it been since he joined her for some naked time in the shower? Months? *A year?* James slung his arm across his face and tugged on the collar of his T-shirt. *Whew.* He knew he and Gwen weren't in the best of ways recently, but did that mean he couldn't enjoy the thought of making love to her right now?

If they hadn't had much sex recently, what did that mean about the kinky side of their relationship? Used to be they were two of the biggest rabble-rousers in the local kink scene. God knew they were the most established couple, thanks in part to James's affable humor and Gwen's ability to talk to *anyone.* That bartender magic had pulled in so many tips and lovers before she met James. He knew. He loved making her talk about it. *She must've been the best in the business if I decided I wanted her the first night I hung out at that place.* The drinks weren't great, and the atmosphere was okay, but Gwen? The lead bartender who practically ran the place when no one else was around? James had gone every chance he had, so he could talk to her and butter her up for at least one night together.

I mean… we fucked against the wall in her break room. That's a good sign, right?

James propped himself up in bed in time for Gwen to march out in her baggy T-shirt and a toothbrush stuck in her mouth. She ignored him in favor of Ross and Rachel in yet another situation in New York. Gwen was the one who first pondered, "*How do these people have shitty jobs and afford apartments like that in New York?*" and made James wonder how the other side truly lived. (He had regretted asking that after Gwen took him to her hometown in rural Pennsylvania.)

"Gwenny," James said with the voice she used to die for. "How about you come get in bed with me after you finish making your breath nice and pretty."

Used to be she would give him a big, silly smile, complete with toothpaste foam spilling from the corners of her mouth and dripping down the front of her shirt. Tonight, however, Gwen turned and went back into the bathroom like a robot with instructions to follow.

James slipped down his pillow with a sigh. He made sure the TV was off before Gwen came back into the bedroom.

"Can I say that you have the best taste in T-shirts?" James didn't know where this big, baggy gray thing came from, but he adored the way it draped on Gwen's lean body. It accentuated her breasts, her ass, and those *hips* he loved more than the hair on her head. Bonus points if it were cold enough to make her nipples poke through the fabric. Tonight, however, James was not so blessed. "Not as good as mine, of course. Then again… wait. That's one of my shirts, right?" For some reason, that cheered him up.

"Is it?" Gwen pushed herself beneath the covers, tossing her hair into a messy bun that may or may not survive the night. It didn't matter what she did – her hair would always be a giant tangle in the morning, *and* she would always be beyond beautiful, bags beneath her eyes and all. James had been a bit shocked to see what she looked like without makeup, but they had been together for seven years, so he must have gotten used to it. "Maybe. I never noticed."

"You stole it from me years ago." James slipped his arm across her chest. When he wasn't rebuffed, he nibbled on her ear and continued, "I let you keep it because you're so cute."

She chuckled. "Flatterer."

Oh, good! This was going well! *I can't believe I'm now so excited when she's open to me flirting with her, let alone in bed.* Well, James was *always* excited to flirt with his domestic partner, but granted Gwen's mood over the past year, it was more like relief than excitement. That little thrill wasn't about possibly getting laid for the first time in two months. It was 100% hoping that Gwen was finally coming around to the new changes in their collective life.

"You know me." He wrapped both arms around her and held her close to his chest. *With any luck, I won't… damnit. There it goes.* His brain said to hold off on arousal, but his cock had other ideas. The ornery thing was anxious to get this party started for the first time in… how long ago had it been when she helped him get to sleep after an anxious night? *A handjob. That's what I'm longing after right now? Kill me. Just kill me, Gwenny.*

"Yes, I know you quite well, Mr. Merange." The way that jumbled name slipped off Gwen's tongue was as good as sex. "Like how you're buttering me up right now to get some."

"Get some what?"

"You know what."

"Nah. Not me. No idea. You gotta use small words to make me understand."

He could feel her roll her eyes. "Don't know what you're talking about."

"Saaaaay it. Say *sexxxxx.*"

"Ew!" Gwen playfully pushed against his chest as she giggled her way out of the bed. "You got spit all over my ear!"

"Not the only place I can put some spit, if you know what I mean."

She was halfway out the bed, shirt riding up her back and showing off her complete lack of underwear. "I'm on my period."

He raised his eyebrows, because after seven years together, James had seen his fair share of period happenings. *I know you just got out of the shower, dear, but I can clearly see your pussy and it's very much not aiding and abetting Aunt Flo.*

"Liar."

Gwen flung herself onto her back. "Maybe."

He lightly smacked her bare thigh, head still propped up on his hand and eyebrows waggling. "Just say you don't want me. It's fine."

Gwen spun onto her side, away from him.

"I'm not falling for that."

"Just trying to have a little fun." James lay down, hands behind his head and smile tugging at the corners of his mouth. "Remember how much fun you used to have when I opened those doors for you?"

"You mean the doors that let you insert your foot into your mouth?"

"That's the one."

Gwen sighed. "You really are good at that."

"I'm good at a *lot* of things." He looped his arm around her waist and brought her closer to him. The perfect opportunity for his cock to hit her bare ass and remember what it wanted. *Look, man, you're not helping my case here. I know you miss our girl, but I have a feeling stabbing her ass isn't going to help us get laid.* For some reason, that didn't work. Which meant James was going to have to go with Plan B.

"Have I told you recently that you are the most beautiful woman in the world?"

Gwen opened her mouth but retracted what she wanted to say. That was good. Because it meant she was rethinking her immediate reaction to an old friend knocking at her back door. *One you haven't said hello to in a while, Gwenny!* If she really were not in the mood, she would have told him to sod off and slammed her head on the pillow. James would have stayed on his side of the bed… and maybe go take another shower.

"Not recently, no. You've been slacking. Starting to think you're about to trade me in for a younger model."

That *almost* offended James, a man once thought to be imperturbable. "Younger? What would I do with a younger woman? Can't get much younger than you, anyway. You're what, twenty-one?"

"Ha, ha," Gwen said, still facing away from him. "Girls who are now my age when we met are from a different generation. I think. When does Millennial end, and Gen Z begin?"

"I have no idea. I refute the idea that I am a Millennial every single day." James was in his thirties, for fuck's sake. He also hated avocados!

"Technically, we are."

"*Technically,* I'd rather be making out than talking about this."

Gwen finally rolled in his direction. "I lied."

"About what?"

"I'm not on my period."

James grinned so widely that he almost pulled a muscle. "Even if you were, my dear, it wouldn't make a lick of difference to me." *Or the friend between my legs. He really, really doesn't care.*

"It'd make a difference to me."

James lightly kissed her shoulder. "I love you, Gwenny."

The way she tensed beneath his touch suggested she hadn't expected him to suddenly sound so soft and sincere. "I love you too, Jimmy."

He laughed. "Touché. Every time." Nobody hated that nickname more than James, who would rather have his two front teeth punched out than ever be called *Jimmy* with any level of sincerity. Still, if he was calling his girlfriend Gwenny, she had every right to throw Jimmy back at him. It had been that way since their first official date and he asked, "*Can I call you Gwenny? I really wanna call you Gwenny.*"

"*Only if I can call you Jimmy,*" she had retorted.

"You mean it?" He spooned her, their bodies molding together as if they had always been that way. "Because I'll always mean it when I say that I love you."

She relaxed in his embrace. "Of course I mean it. You think I'm the type of woman to lie about loving someone? What do you think I want from you? Your money?"

"Think you want my cock, honestly."

"Your money is flashy and temperamental, but your cock is forever."

"Aw, but you'd still love me if I like… lost my cock, right?"

"James Merange," Gwen said with a sigh, before she turned over in his embrace and lightly slapped his cheek. "You are the only man I have ever met who could say that with a straight face."

"My face ain't straight."

"Not much about you is."

He hooked his hand on his hip. "Still talking about my cock, are we?"

She felt him up within his loose-fitting sweatpants. "Uh huh."

"Woo boy, you woke him up now." James wasn't kidding, either. It had been mind over matter before now. He'd be lucky to make it another few minutes without throwing himself on Gwen. "What are you going to do about that?"

"Would you come out and say you want to fuck me?"

"I'm *trying* to be suave. It's been a while, okay? I'm rusty."

"You better not be rusty with this thing."

"Is that… is that the go ahead I've been waiting for all this time?" James rolled onto his back again, arms spread wide and mouth agape in wonder. "I can't believe it. Finally. The moment I've been praying for. Just ask my priest."

"I'm not asking priests anything about you."

With a smile that announced his impure intentions, James flung himself onto his partner, grunting in glee as she yelped in giggly surprise.

If there was one thing he could say about their relationship, it was that it had always felt *right.* When James walked into Gwen's bar that first night, tired from work and questioning the direction his life was heading, he beheld a warm light that invited him into quirky conversations and brought with it the knowledge that he had found The One he had been searching for.

Because, unlike what some people liked to spout about James' college years, he had always been a big ol' romantic at heart.

If there was anything he wanted to impart to Gwen that night, it was the sense of longing he still harbored in his heart. She was the only woman who had ever seen him for who he really was. While James may have been the only heir to a vast fortune, he was also an easy-going guy who would rather have fun with real people in a dingy dive bar than spend his evenings in gentlemen's clubs, networking and greasing wheels. He also enjoyed the finer things, as his upbringing dictated. He needed a woman who understood an emotionally simpler life while also not batting her pretty eyelashes at hopping a plane to Kenya at the last minute. Gwen had become that woman in such a short amount of time. Every day James considered himself the luckiest man in the world.

Which was why he was determined to keep her. Forever.

I know you're thinking about leaving me. James was more in tune with her thoughts and feelings than she may have ever thought. It was what kept their relationship fresh – up until the baby made things a little *too* fresh. *I don't want you to ever leave me. I would understand if you did, but… I can't allow it.* James had an arduous task before him. Either convince Gwen that it was always worth staying with him…

Or cut his losses. Now.

That was impossible. Gwen was too precious to ever cut off.

She probably wanted a nice, hot quickie to sate whatever needs had been building up within her body for the past few weeks. Both of their moods were amicable to having sex like they used to. But James knew that a hit it and quit it on a Monday night wouldn't be enough to give Gwen endless thoughts of how much he loved her – and why she should stay.

"Do you know how much I love you?" James wrapped his arms tightly around her torso, holding Gwen's limbs to her side and making her ass wiggle against his pelvis. "I love you so much that I'm never going to let you go. Especially not tonight."

James was a guy who liked to workout. That was one of the best ways to socialize with some of his closest friends. What guy didn't like hitting the gym or the track with one of his best friends to spot him and shoot the breeze? The guys he went with changed with the breezes, but one thing always remained the same: James's physique. He didn't have rippling muscles or washboard abs, but he was fit, tough, and *strong.* Gwen hit the gym on the regular basis too, and God knew she could uppercut an attacker in the jaw, but she was no match for James when he wanted to make a point in the bedroom. Feeling her wiggle like that, as she assessed whether she could make a game of trying to free herself from her gasp, was half the fun of making love.

They had a safe word as old as their relationship. *Vermillion. The name of the bar where we met.* If Gwen really didn't want to deal with his games, she would utter it in a heartbeat. She had done it before. That ruthless color had killed more than a few moods over the years, and James held his breath that it wouldn't happen tonight. *Want me, Gwen. Still want me.*

Her body stiffened in his grasp. His cock strained against his sweatpants, eager to have some fun and score some relief. Yet James would never in a million years push her to do something she didn't want.

"Good," she whispered, inviting him to wrap his whole body around hers and to nestle his lips against her ear. "Maybe I don't want to be let go."

That was the thing about Gwen. She was a tough girl who knew how to take punches and hurl them right back. It was what made her so resilient to the shit she put up with in her partner's world, a world she never knew existed until they met. Gwen was no wilting flower. She was a strong, unbending tree that swayed with the winds and bloomed even when her branches were tangled by the seasonal storms. That was the kind of woman James needed in his life. He wasn't about to let her go.

Not when she kept him so steadfastly in the moment. Like now, when she gasped to have him touch her beneath her shirt and search for her wetness. He momentarily feared that she wouldn't want him after all. He had blessedly been wrong.

Sometimes, when he made love to the love of his life, he wondered what it would be like to want *more.* More than this. More than what people saw when James Merange and Gwen Mitchell walked into a room, hand-in-hand. More than the silly rumors about the kinky sex life they now rarely indulged.

"You want this, don't you?" James rocked into her from behind. It was easy enough to talk when his words voiced everything going through his head, from how soft she felt to his touch, to how beautiful her moans were. "Tell me how much you want it."

Gwen shoved her face into the pillow, a long, drawn-out moan eliciting the kind of attention they both craved. It would be a miracle if James could hold off climax for more than another minute. Weeks since they last made love? Desperately wanting her? Living in the moment and foregoing a scripted scene? Miracles could happen, but he wasn't praying for one right now.

"Give it to me."

Her sweet groan was all James needed. He held her close, touched her body, and gave her exactly what they both wanted.

It was the harried kind of love that was full of intent and divine purpose. James could easily imagine spending the rest of his life with this woman. From the moment he first kissed her, he knew that was his end-game.

Him. Gwen. Whatever life they carved out together. He didn't care what kind it was, as long as they had fun and were happy. It was that attitude that had led them on many adventures and opened their hearts and minds to certain things other couples balked at.

Then again, that had always been James's attitude toward life. He was the son of stuffy rich parents who *didn't* turn out like them, much to their chagrin.

Damnit. He wasn't supposed to think about them right now. He was only supposed to think about Gwen, and how good she felt.

"Come for me, Gwen." James was on the edge, but he could hold off a while longer if it meant Gwen stole the show for a second. Besides, what felt better than a woman climaxing on his cock?

Love, perhaps. Those often went together for James Merange.

"I'm coming," Gwen gasped, voice still muffled by her pillow. James shoved his face between the locks of her hair and kissed the back of her neck. It offered him more leverage as Gwen shimmied from him with her oncoming orgasm. He had to find *some* way to pin her down and make her accept what he had to offer. "I'm…"

James may have been on top and in control, but Gwen was the one suffocating him with nothing but her inner walls. Because there she went, clamping onto his cock and bringing him down from his mighty, lofty heights. She cried out in ecstasy, her harried *Oh-oh-ohs* growing louder until she rode an untouchable cloud James could only hope to match.

"*Fuck*." The point of no return had arrived. James flung himself on top of her and shoved himself as deep as he could go. But his thrusts had ceased, for his brain was too consumed with the heat of pleasure to keep up with his movements.

"Oh, God." Gwen's mouth was open, and her eyes closed. Her body stretched against his, left leg curling tighter around his so she was completely open and accepting of his lovemaking. James languished in the slow waves of orgasm taking over. Never had there been a time in their relationship when Gwen didn't allow him inside her like this. "That's unreal."

James chuckled into the crook of her neck. Here came the fatigue, and he was willing to wallow in it. "You're unreal."

"You say that *every* time."

"I wouldn't want to disappoint you, Gwen."

He rolled onto his back, hand on his face to keep out the offensive light still on in their bedroom. Gwen slowly shifted toward him and took up residence in the turn of his arm.

"You never have."

A ball of her hair ended up in his fist. James sighed. "We'll get through this. We get through everything."

Gwen closed her eyes. "I don't want to talk about that."

"What do you want to do, then?"

"Lay here."

So they did, for a few minutes, at least.

CHAPTER 5

GWEN

Gwen was jealous of women who had *purpose.* Like Kathryn and her endless charitable pursuits, or Charlotte and those tawdry stories she uploaded to Amazon under a pen name.

Not that Gwen didn't enjoy her life. Yet when Ophelia Merange called Gwen to ask her to tea at the country club that Friday afternoon, Gwen wished she had a reason to get out of it. "*Sorry, I have an important work meeting that day.*" "*Sorry, I'm donating my eggs to women in fertile need.*" "*Sorry, I'm rebuilding houses in Puerto Rico.*" "*Sorry, I'm baking pancakes for orphans.*" The only thing Gwen had planned for Friday was hitting the gym. Gwen wasn't an athlete, but she enjoyed spending a couple hours a day at the local gym enjoying badminton with friends.

Too bad that wasn't good enough. Gwen agreed to meet with a sigh on her lips and a palpitation of her heart. While she didn't dislike James's mother, she *was* her own special little trip to attend.

Gwen selected a long-sleeved navy-blue dress and pulled her hair into a tight ponytail that put only a *little* bit of strain on her neck. It was a blander look than she preferred for her daily life, but the country club – let alone Ophelia's company – asked for more traditional, stuffier looks that made Gwen feel like she was attending her own funeral. When she asked Rebecca to phone a taxi after lunch, Gwen decided she would go back up to her room and redo her makeup to darker shades instead of the sapphire blue she would normally wear with this dress.

She sat at her vanity, arms wrapped around her torso. Coming into this room, with its fresh memories of what she and James had accomplished over several years, was sometimes difficult to bear.

I almost fell in love with him all over again Monday night. Almost. Gwen had been cautious about sparing too many feelings for her partner until she knew for sure what outcome was best for their relationship. But being made love to like that reaffirmed that James still harbored much affection for her. The fact they woke up yesterday morning and spent an extra half hour in bed so they could fool around didn't help, either. *I told myself no more throwing my mouth at his cock, but there I was, chopping down the morning wood.* Gwen needed to figure shit out, and quickly.

She supposed seeing Ophelia and perhaps asking her advice would help. Lady Merange had always been Gwen's biggest ally in the Merange family, after James, of course.

The taxi pulled up before the gates. The guard asked to see her membership card, and while he scanned the chip, she leaned forward to pay her driver. "This is fine," she asserted. Really, it wasn't, since she would have to borrow a golf cart from the gatehouse to drive the rest of the way to the main country club house, but that was less of a hassle than dealing with a lost taxi driver running around aimlessly on private property.

"I'm supposed to meet Lady Ophelia Merange in the tearoom," Gwen said to the guard after getting out of the taxi. "Do you know if she's here yet?"

"Mr. Weathersby at the concierge desk will help you get situated with that, ma'am." The guard handed back her card and motioned her toward the lineup of golf carts. "Do you require assistance?"

"No, thank you." Gwen hopped into the closest cart. Her Prada heels were caught beneath the pedal, but she pretended nothing was amiss as she cheerily smiled at the guard and waved the taxi driver off. "Do let them know I'm on my way, though." He would do that anyway. It was one of his primary functions!

Fifteen minutes later, after nearly mowing over the bushes lining the country club driveway and scaring a landscaper half to death when she took a corner too quickly, Gwen was inside the main house and led to the sunny tearoom on the second floor of the mansion.

Ophelia was already there, reading the paper and sipping her Bombay Breakfast and munching on her macarons. She stood up when Gwen entered the otherwise empty tearoom and offered to kiss her cheeks in greeting.

Ophelia had aged considerably since Gwen first met her. Gone was the soft auburn of her hair, replaced by strands of silver threads that now crowned her as a matriarch of an old and revered New England clan. Her hands had wrinkled and shook when she didn't eat enough, which was often, since the Merange family doctor claimed Ophelia was now prone to "fits," as he old-fashionedly put it. Gwen knew the signs of anxiety. Most of the bartenders she knew had loads of it.

Hard to believe Ophelia was barely in her sixties. She looked at least seventy, albeit sophisticatedly so.

"Do try the Appalachian Summer they just received," Ophelia said with her wispy voice. Gwen looked up from the tea menu with a quizzical expression. "Tea, dear. They don't get much of it, but it's heavenly."

They made the usual small talk while they had their tea and Gwen indulged in the excellent cucumber sandwiches the country club made on site. It made up for the light lunch she ate back home, which Ophelia was sure to ask about, since she adored the Colonial manor her son bought a few years ago.

"You should come by and see what your son has done with his home office," Gwen said with a sigh. "Looks like one of Albert's."

"Then I don't need to see. I already know what it will look like." Ophelia gently brushed aside a silver lock of hair hanging in her face. "Let me guess. Brazenly dark oaken walls and floors, ebony black or forest green throw rugs, and enough amber-hued spirits to make you wonder how he gets any work done in there."

"That about sums it up." Ophelia had left out James's obsession with christening the renovations with a hot and heavy copulation session on his leather couch, though. Then again, maybe she hadn't, but had the manners to keep her speculations on her son's sex life to herself.

"He takes too much after his father sometimes. Hopefully in only the right ways."

Ophelia wouldn't make eye contact when she said that, as if she were ashamed to think that her son might be too much like her husband. Most of the affluent matriarchs in Gwen's circles would rather die than think they had begotten children nothing like their fathers. DNA testing may have been a readily available thing in the twenty-first century, but traditional mothers always feared their paranoid husbands would find outrageous grounds to divorce them.

What was Ophelia's deal in her marriage? Anything she wanted, as long as she looked the other way while her husband conducted a clandestine affair with Madam Welsh over the span of *decades?* Some of the most disgusting things Gwen had heard over the past year were whispers that Cassandra was actually Albert's daughter, meaning the child she had with James's sperm was incest at its best.

Madam Welsh would have never, though. She would ensure her only child was her spouse's and *then* get freaky with another woman's husband.

Gwen felt sorry for Ophelia. They were both black sheep, albeit for different reasons.

"Have you seen my grandson recently?" Ophelia asked during a lull in their conversation.

Gwen swallowed the last of her tea. "Can't say I have, no."

"He's growing *so* big. Reminds me of James at that age. Baby boys sprout up like little dandelions. Can be quite weedy like them as well." Ophelia chuckled. "He's such a cutie-pie. Makes me wish he had come into this world under better circumstances."

"Yet you knew what the Welshes had done." Gwen hadn't meant to sound so accusatory, but how could she avoid it when the topic always angered her?

Ophelia poured the last of her tea from her small China pot. The hand-painted wisteria blooms would have once amazed Gwen, had she not become so jaded to the sort of affluence infecting everything she now touched. *Sometimes I miss the days of getting my hands dirty in a middle-class bar.* Hell, she would even take a dive bar sometimes. At least she didn't have to adopt a new set of manners there.

"I did." Ophelia had never denied it. She would've been foolish to claim ignorance, since her name was also on the papers saying the Welshes could use her son's damned sperm. "I regret it, though. Then again, I regretted it the moment the papers were filed."

"Because you did it behind James's back."

"Yes." Ophelia swallowed. "I wanted to talk to you today about the men in my family. From one outsider to another."

Outsider? In what universe was Ophelia a true outsider? Her family had gobs of money, although their reign as the kings of the New England lumber industry had ended when the first of many mills closed in the late early seventies. Ophelia's family had been quick to arrange a marriage with Albert Merange before the money ran out. They had done it for her sisters, too, and now all four of them could say they had married into more money than their family could currently claim. As the oldest of her sisters, Ophelia had dibs on the most lucrative match, even though everyone knew Albert was in love with Sarah Holliday and often had premarital honeymoons with her all over Europe. There were even rumors that they had eloped before Albert's marriage to Ophelia, but they were never proven and always denied.

Gwen supposed Ophelia meant that she was an outsider in the mental sense. She had always been a *guest* in the Merange household. A promise fulfilled to old family friends. She pumped out one baby boy and sealed her place in the Merange legacy. She never wanted for money, healthcare, or excuses to travel the world. Love? That was another story.

"From the time James was a boy, Albert had lobbied for us to arrange a marriage with the little Welsh girl. I told him that was terribly old-fashioned – it was the nineties, you know. Even if we *had* arranged a marriage, it wouldn't be legally binding, and James would do as he pleased as he already does." Ophelia shrugged. "Like his father!"

"I'm sorry." That was all Gwen could say about that.

"It's all right."

"Besides, I already knew that Albert and Sarah conspired to get their kids married. James has told me plenty of times, especially over this past year."

"I'm sure he heard us talking a time or two. James likes to pretend he's carefree, but he has a sharp wit, as I'm sure you've noticed. Anyway, I proposed we let them become playmates and hope that a natural romance may bloom between them as they grew up. Albert was, of course, for the idea, which is how James and Cassandra became close friends until recent years."

"He's been quite distraught by her behavior." That was an understatement. James always expressed apprehension over his childhood friend's promiscuity, since he claimed it didn't come from a genuine place. "*She's using sex as a band-aid for something deeply troubling her,*" James said after rumors flew about Cassandra frequenting a local pleasure house. "*I worry about her well-being. It's like she's one more boyfriend away from a meltdown.*" Apparently, Cassandra's problem was that James wasn't interested in her after she had pined after him like a silly girl for years. "I would be surprised if they repaired their friendship after so much distrust."

Ophelia's eyes were sharper than Gwen had ever seen them. "I know it hasn't been easy for you, either. I'm so sorry, Gwenyth."

"Yes, well…" Gwen wouldn't play the games that somehow absolved Ophelia from her role in this mess. Even if Lady Merange had little choice but to support her husband and his real love in this distasteful endeavor, she still did it knowing how much her son and his girlfriend would be harmed in the process. Greed. Selfishness. Those very things they claimed to fight in their children's generation. "It *has* been difficult. James and I are not the same as we used to be, though I understand he knew nothing of these machinations."

"It can't be easy. My son doesn't talk to me about these things, but I know he's vented frustrations to his father." That was probably an understatement. Gwen had witnessed James ripping his own father a new asshole over his role in this charade. "*The fact that man would rather have a bastard grandson he ripped from my nuts than anything we might have, Gwenny… I can't forgive him.*" She had believed James when he said that, too. *I had never seen him so angry before.* James wasn't a man prone to anger. When he popped, it was because some great injustice had been thrust upon the people he loved.

Ophelia folded her hands on the table.

"I asked you here today," she began, sighing, "because I wanted to talk about your future with my son."

Gwen did not pale. Nor did her breath hitch in her chest. The only thing giving away her apprehension was her drying throat, and Ophelia could not see that. "I had always considered you one of my biggest supporters, Lady Merange." Fat lot of good it did Gwen when Ophelia carried so little power in her family. Meant one less person to give her shit during Christmas.

"Which is why I am invested in your well-being, dear. My son's happiness is my happiness. Your happiness is his happiness. Therefore, your happiness is my happiness."

Gwen couldn't help but smile a little. "I appreciate that."

"You may not have been the woman I would have chosen for my son," Ophelia continued, sure to cut Gwen off before she could protest, "but that doesn't mean James has poor taste. I've seen you two together for years. I understand what he sees in you."

Gwen sat back. "You do?"

"Of course, dear. You laugh at his terrible jokes and have always been by his side, including through this ordeal. That's something a mother truly appreciates. The fact you're *very* pretty is something he must appreciate as well."

"Thank you."

"That said, I completely understand if this is the final straw for you and you wish to cut ties from my son."

Gwen said nothing.

"Since I've seen you two together for so long, I can also see the signs of your relationship falling apart. This distresses me, because I know how much my son has invested in making you his life partner."

Not sure you know how much, Lady Merange. "There has been much in the way of obstacles in our relationship as of late."

"Of course. I simply want you to know that I understand and am here for whatever decision you make."

"Whatever… decision?"

"If you wish to stay with my son and perhaps one day marry him… I will support that, even if my husband may be displeased. Yet if you wish to cut ties and move on with your life, dear, I will also understand that. You're in the most impossible position in all of this. Not even James could argue that."

Gwen wouldn't argue that, either.

"I'll be frank. My husband has never approved of you once it became clear our son was madly in love with you – and you returned his ardor with the fervor only a mother can see. My husband and I have fought over your relationship more than anything else in our marriage." Ophelia looked down at her lap, as if she couldn't believe she was about to admit the following. "Including his affair. Somehow, that was easier to swallow than him forbidding his own son's happiness like his parents forbade his."

The tearoom overseer quietly approached the table and asked if Gwen and Ophelia required anything. Ophelia politely yet curtly asked him to leave them be. When a trio of middle-aged women entered the tearoom to have their afternoon sustenance, Ophelia called the overseer back and asked him to sit them as far away as possible. With a nod of the head, the man showed the bubbly, talkative women to the far corner by the sunlit windows. They thought themselves most fortunate to have such a private, beautiful table. It kept them from overhearing the intimate conversation on the other side of the salon. And it prevented Gwen and Ophelia from having to hear the details of horse breeding and racing.

"I know you do not ask my opinion," Gwen said, "but I feel that your husband is using James to relive the life he wished he had with Sarah Welsh."

Ophelia did not flinch to hear this truth. "He is. I've accused him of such many times."

What was it like to be trapped in her unhealthy marriage? When she was married off at such a young age, she must have felt such a burden to help her family. Coupled with the era she grew up in, what choice did she have? Now, when support would be greater for her leaving a philandering husband, she was much older and had none of her own money or life skills to support herself. *I could never be like that.* Gwen didn't have to be, though. She grew up in a different age with a different set of standards. Her parents would be happy if she carved out a half-decent living for herself, let alone anyone else!

"James has made it clear that he loves you and not Cassandra. I see no reason to not allow you into our family. The role I played in recent events… I'm not proud of them. But I hope you can forgive me."

"I'm sure you had little power in the situation."

"Yes, well… nothing a woman likes to admit, of course."

Gwen mangled the napkin in her lap. Something gnawed at her, begging her to say the one thing she had been keeping locked in her heart for the past two – or was it three? – years. But when she and James made a secret promise to one another, they had agreed to not tell *anyone* what they had done. No one. Not their parents. Not their best friends. Nobody.

A secret just for them.

"I won't lie to you," Gwen said, looking up again. "I have entertained many fantasies of leaving your son this past year. What has happened has been a great strain on not only our relationship, but our own health."

Ophelia sighed, absorbing much of the blame. "But you love him, of course."

"It's not as easy as me packing my bags and going home, or wherever else I may please."

Something in Gwen's tone must have roused Ophelia's full attention, for now both women locked gazes as if nothing else was more important than what Gwen had to say.

If she could bring herself to say it. After all, it meant breaking one of her old promises to James, and she had weighed how much it mattered to her now.

Or how much it mattered to anyone, even him.

CHAPTER 6

JAMES

"I fold." James tossed his poker hand onto the table and leaned back to sip his cognac. It didn't come close to bourbon on a scale of *It's acceptable* to *I'd rather drink my own piss,* but when a man was at a country club, he didn't have much choice in the matter. The old guard passed out cognac. He would bloody well drink cognac.

His best friend Ian Mathers hooted in surprise when it turned out he won that round of poker with nothing but two pairs. James grumbled that the dealer had been shoddy, but he soon realized he meant himself. *Me. I'm the dealer.*

Cognac and poker was the flavor of the day at the monthly meeting for Beta Kappa Phi, the fraternity most of the city's well-bred males joined once they reached undergrad at select universities. (If a man was well-bred enough, there were only a few undergrads he could attend. That went double for men like James and Ian, who were the only children of their families' great business ventures.) The fact most of the old brothers lived in the same city only leant to them meeting up once a month to relive those so-called glory days.

Gwen was here yesterday, wasn't she? James thanked his lucky star that his mother didn't ask to see Gwen on a Saturday, when her husband and son would be tearing up the lounge with their old frat buddies. The cigar and cigarette smoke alone were enough to kill the sensitive lungs in the room. Luckily, that was mostly relegated to the balcony area, and James was free to breathe in the far corner of the room where the poker games were afoot.

He didn't have time to ponder what his mother and Gwen had talked about the day before. Not when Ian demanded another round, complete with his chips piling high before him.

"You're going to clean me out." James didn't gamble often, but when he did, he made sure to gamble no more than ten thousand. That was enough, since that was a mid-range weekend vacation with Gwen. If he lost all his money? Oh, well. He supposed that meant they were staying in for the weekend. Whatever *would* they do? "How am I supposed to explain to Gwen that I'm a poor man if you feel it in your heart to steal my last dime?"

Ian shuffled the cards. Probably injected an extra ace in there. "I don't need your money, Jim. I need your soul."

"So *that's* how you stay looking so good in your thirties?"

"Says the man as old as me."

James stacked his chips into a wobbly tower. "You're the one known for your ghastly good looks. I always had a different method for charming the ladies."

"You think my looks were good enough to bed as many women as I have?" Ian clicked his tongue as he dealt the cards for another round of poker. "You have to be charming, you fool. That's the one thing you're probably better at than I am."

"We all have our strengths."

Ian downed the last of his cognac before looking at his hand. "Ah, shit."

"I'm not falling for that."

"Nah. It's bad. You've got this one."

"You haven't even exchanged cards yet."

They played through two more hands, James losing every one. *My head isn't in the game.* All he could think about was Gwen, and how she joined him for dinner at home the night before with only a sullen tug of her lips.

"What's wrong with you?" Ian pushed the cards to the side when James lost his fifth hand in a row. "You're usually not this bad at poker."

"I'm usually not this distracted."

Ian opened his mouth but closed it as quickly. Probably because whatever he wanted to say was uncouth enough to get a smack across that mouth. Instead, he cleared his throat, finished stacking the cards and chips, and said, "How's the kid?"

James shot him a look that implied he knew Ian really meant, *How's Gwen?* That was the problem with knowing someone for as long as he knew Ian. The two of them had been inseparable since they rushed Beta Kappa Phi together. Ian was the first person to learn about Gwen's existence after James left that bar with her face imprinted on his memory. "*There's this girl at that bar on the other side of town. Vermillion, I think it's called. Ever been there? Hottest bartender I've ever seen.*" Ian didn't bother remembering Gwen's face or name until James swore he had never been so in love.

That was years ago. Since then, James had seen his best friend go through a string of women until finally hooking up with Kathryn, the one woman he had wanted since he was a horny teenager. *Yes, he told me all the embarrassing stories.* In college, no less, when they were so drunk during midterms that James shared his homoerotic fantasies and Ian confessed he once tried to hook up with Kathryn, but prematurely… arrived. *Crazy to think that back then, those were deep, dark secrets we both kept.* Aging and maturity had granted them some perspective.

"He's getting big." James dug into his pocket before the inevitable follow-up question arrived. "Saw him on Monday, and he was as big as a preschooler." That was an overstatement, but James couldn't hide the bit of pride that hit him when he realized his genetics contributed to that. *That doesn't make sense. I can't control my genetics. I didn't even control his creation.* Sometimes, the male ego didn't have to make sense, let alone to the man in possession of such an ego. "Look at him." James passed his phone to Ian. An album of Patrick's pictures and videos were ready for swiping. "Looks like me, doesn't he?"

That wasn't surprising. First thing James did after hearing Cassandra's confession was order a paternity test. When it came back positive, he resigned himself to this sudden fatherhood.

"Good Lord. He really does." Ian swallowed his next observation.

"Go on. Say it. I know what you're thinking, man."

Ian shook his head. "He looks exactly like you and Cassandra."

That also wasn't surprising, since James and Cassandra both possessed dark hair and similar facial features. Those facts helped fuel the rumors that they shared the same father. Luckily for them, Patrick's paternity test had also debunked the rumors that he was inbred, not that either the Meranges or the Welshes needed proof of *that.*

"Beautiful kid, James." Ian swiped through some of the photos, most of them taken as recently as that Monday. "You've gotta be proud."

"I am. I want to do right by that kid, you know."

"Of course you do. I hope the Welshes aren't stonewalling you."

James considered that for a moment. "They've been quite accommodating at including me in my own son's life, although Sarah made sure I knew I had little say in his upbringing. Unless I wanted to make him my heir, of course."

"Well? Aren't you?"

"Aren't I what?"

Ian cocked his head. "Making him your heir. I thought you and Gwen weren't having kids, and you're gonna need an heir."

"I'm sure that's what they're hoping for. I haven't decided yet. Would rather see how he turns out, you know?"

"Of course."

James could've used the opportunity to flip the script on Ian. Maybe goad him about what *he* would do about heirs, since Kathryn was not the baby begetting type. Even if the Alison family died out with her – since God knew they didn't do anything with their money anymore – there were still the Mathers, who had a healthy and thriving hospitality company. Ian was set to take that over, but where did that leave future generations? It was a conundrum James was too familiar with.

But James was too absorbed in his thoughts to play games with Ian. "I'm worried about Gwen," he said.

Ian sighed, as if he had known that was coming. "She doesn't look that happy anymore."

"Can you blame her?"

"No. Now she knows for sure that your family hates her."

"She's always known that. Besides, my mom doesn't hate her. My mom's too spineless to do anything about how my father treats Gwen. That's why I have to pull double-duty on that front."

"Sorry to hear that."

"Yeah, well…" Ian didn't understand. His parents *loved* Kathryn, and her father was quite fond of him. He rarely dealt with the kind of familial drama that resulted in destroyed bonds and terrible rumors that haunted children for life. *Do you know what it's like for everyone to know your dad's fucking some other married woman? Do you know what it's like for people to joke that you're half-siblings with the mother of your child?* James had walked into many rooms of quieted laughter that past year. He knew he was the object of every joke. "I think Gwen's gonna leave me."

"Nah. No way."

James tapped his forehead against the card table. "You don't get it. I'm not sure how we're going to get past what's happened. She's like this otherworldly creature now. I see her, I hear her, God knows I feel her vibes every time we're in the same room… but I can't penetrate the veil she's drawn. I think she's girding herself for breaking up with me. Cut me off now so it doesn't hurt as much when she actually does it."

"She knows this shit isn't your fault, right? She can't possibly think you actually had an affair with Cassandra." Was that a hiss in Ian's voice?

"You say that like you didn't enjoy dating her."

"There's a reason I broke up with her."

"She dumped *you.*"

Ian shrugged. "It wouldn't have worked out. She's the wrong kind of emotionally volatile for me." He grinned. "I like my mates running themselves ragged because they're overachievers, as you may have noticed. Lot easier to get *those* kinds to calm down."

"Cassandra is volatile, all right." Volatile enough to think it was a good idea to steal her childhood friend's sperm and ride off with his baby. "She's lucky I don't want to fight for custody. I would make her life such hell if I wanted. Probably kill her." James didn't say that with any joy. The thought of doing that to a woman he once held so dear hurt his poor, empathetic heart. *Dad always did say my ability to feel things would be the end of me.* Albert would know all about that.

"Why didn't you ever go out with her?" Ian asked. "God knows everyone thought it would happen before you ended up with Gwen."

"Are you asking from a place of genuine curiosity?"

"Naturally."

James held up one of his chips, the edges tickling her fingertips as it rolled between his thumb and forefinger. "It wasn't ever like that with her. We grew up together. Some people see growing up together as a precursor for romance, and guys like me… well, those girls become sisters, not dates." He put the chip down. "In another life, if I were still single and she was desperate…"

"Yeah?"

"All she had to do was ask, and I probably would have made that baby with her. Just not the old-fashioned way."

"I see."

"Yeah." James glanced over his shoulder and caught sight of his father on the balcony, having a cigar and laughing it up with men his age. "Gwen changed everything, I guess."

"Hey, if you guys break up, it's not only your hearts that will be broken. You've got a bunch of fans, my friend."

James tossed the chip into the air and caught it with his fist. "Don't think your heart compares in any way to mine."

"I remember when you were one of the most noncommittal men I had ever met."

The same could be said about you. Kathryn had changed that for Ian, who had been crowned the city's biggest playboy before he fell in love. "Like I said." James let the chip in his hand fall to the floor. "Gwen changed everything."

***

He approached her from behind, careful to make sure she acknowledged his presence before he wrapped his arms around her.

"Let's go somewhere tomorrow," he said. "I don't have anything going on Monday until the early evening, so we could spend the night somewhere. How about it? We could drive up to New York or fly down to Miami. What's your poison, lovely?"

Gwen scoffed, buttoning up the rest of her sleep shirt. It was like she firmly said, "*We are not having sex tonight.*" Last Monday had been a fluke, apparently. And the fooling around they did a couple days later… didn't that mean something? Apparently not.

"Can't say either New York or Miami appeal to me right now."

"Then where do you want to go?" James gently rocked her back and forth, careful to keep his awakening manhood from making a fool of them both. "We could rent that cabin in the mountains. You remember the one. From our ho…"

"It's too cold for that," Gwen snapped. "What if it's snowing up there?"

"Fine. Let's at least go out to dinner tomorrow. I know it's Sunday, but The Dark Hour might have something fun going on."

Gwen gently freed herself from his grasp and sat at her vanity, where she brushed a few tangles out of her long hair. James pried his eyes from how her sleep shirt clung to her torso. The highlight of her breasts was *not* helping him seduce her. Not when all he could think about was getting her in bed, preferably on her hands and knees. The sex-starved parts of his brain wanted it hard and fast. And to pull her hair…

They hadn't been that wild in months. James recalled a time when they were considered the kinkiest couple in town, because there was barely a thing they wouldn't try. Bondage and power plays were only the tips of the iceberg. Everyone at the BDSM club had seen them naked more than once, and it didn't bother James any more than everyone seeing him limp after twisting his ankle at the gym.

Those were the real glory days of his youth. Every time he and Gwen did something outrageous or brought a smile to some stranger's face were the memories he wanted to treasure until his dying day.

How could he make her see that?

"You don't want to go anywhere?" he asked her.

Gwen hesitated on her twentieth brush stroke. "Not really. Maybe when it gets warmer."

"Yeah." James sighed. "Warmer."

The definition of warm was making love in front of the fire. Or laying half-naked in the sunlight on some white, pristine beach somewhere in the world. Either way, they better be sweaty and naked. *Are those jungle treehouses still renting down in Costa Rica, or were they wiped out in the last storm?* Now there was an idea. James had enough money to pay everyone to look the other way while he and Gwen ran around in their birthday suits.

He turned toward the bed. Gwen put her hairbrush down and said, "I really did like that cabin in the woods. It was cozy, but still had all the comforts you've spoiled me with these past few years."

James met her halfway across the bedroom, Gwen's hair down and her body bedecked in shorts and that blasted button-up shirt she wore in winter. *How many times have I unbuttoned it for you, Gwenny?* "Me too. To think, we found it on a total whim after we hopped in my car and asked Siri where the hell we should go."

"Siri always comes through. She's like the third-wheel around here."

"I thought that was Rebecca."

Gwen chuckled. "I'm not asking her where to buy lube when I'm on the other side of town."

"Who are you lubing it up with these days?"

"Your ass."

"I think I would remember that."

Gwen grinned. Then, as if she hadn't meant to show that level of mirth around her partner, she turned away, frowning.

"Nobody loves you like I do, Gwen."

She bristled. "What's that for?"

"Just reminding you."

"You make it sound like I don't know."

James leaned against her vanity, arms crossed. "What's wrong with saying how much I love you every day for the rest of your life? You make it sound like I'm gaslighting you or something."

"That's not what gaslighting is."

"Are *you* the one gaslighting me about what gaslighting means now?"

"Not in the mood for jokes right now, James."

He sighed. "I worry about us, you know."

She said nothing.

"This whole baby thing… I know it's messed with you more than it has with me, and I'm the surprise dad."

"Do you have to bring this up right now?"

"Yes."

Gwen slid her elbows across her vanity until they met the bottom of her mirror. Hands smacked against her face. Fingers pushed into her hair. "Now's really not a good time to talk about it. I'm…"

"You should come with me next week to see Patrick."

His interruption ensured that there were no more words spoken for a whole minute. Slowly, Gwen removed her hands from her face, both eyes looking at her partner as if he had asked her to marry his father.

"How can you ask me that?" she hissed. "God, James, sometimes I swear you're the most tone-deaf person I know."

"I want him to get to know you," James continued. "The earlier he understands how it is in his family, the better. I keep worrying that the family is telling him that his mother and I are together. I know kids can't really get things that young…"

"Trust me, James, they do. You think I didn't understand that my parents divorced when I was three and I had a new dad a year later? Kids are smart. They pick up on everything."

"Exactly. I want to make sure my son picks up on the right things." James would be damned if the Welshes were telling his son that Mommy and Daddy were married. He didn't put it past them. If they were diabolical enough to do what they had, then James had his work cut out for him in the fatherhood department. *I don't want to have to fight for custody, but I will if I think my son is being brainwashed by those heathens.* James hadn't signed away his parental rights, and he wouldn't. Cassandra could marry the top lawyer in the state, and James would go to the next state over and hire *their* top lawyer to get him even half-time custody.

Gwen finally looked at him. Her eyes were dull and sleepy, yet James knew her fatigue came more from the pain in her heart than the wear on her body. "What are you going to do when he's finally old enough to understand how he came to be? What do you think that is going to do to a kid?" Gwen pointed her head back down to her crossed arms on her vanity. "What if we had kids? How would we explain that to them?"

James raised his eyebrows. Gwen brought up children so infrequently, that hearing those words uttered from her lips was like surviving whiplash. "Got something you wanna share, Gwenny?"

"I'm not pregnant."

"I didn't mean that."

She sighed. "I don't know if I'm cut out to be a stepmother. Not to a kid that came about like that." Her hands formed into angry fists. "It would've been bad enough if some unknown baby mama came out of the woodwork… you know, one you actually slept with before you met me. Hell, sometimes I think I would handle you cheating on me better than… *this*."

"If I had cheated on you," James began, knowing that he poked the hornet's nest, "you'd have grounds to break up with me. Cleanly. No judgment from anyone." He walked toward their bed. "That's what you'd love, right? A clean breakup."

"Watch it."

"Watch what?" James flopped onto the bed, hands behind his head. "Our relationship deteriorate because shit got real and hard?"

"It's gotten 'real' before, asshole."

"Yes, and you remember what we did when it got *real*."

Gwen kept her focus on the mirror in front of her. "What clean breakup are you talking about? We lost our chance at that two years ago."

James rolled away from her, facing the empty side of the bed usually reserved for Gwen's form. "I wish you'd talk to me about what's really bothering you. I want to work through this. I need you by my side, Gwen. You're the only one with enough bite in my corner."

"I've been trying for a whole year. I'm tired."

"If you want to break up, fucking say so."

She said nothing. He expected as much.

When Gwen finally came to bed ten minutes later, the lights were off and the ceiling fan turning on its highest setting. James waited until Gwen had settled in before scooting up behind her and saying, "I love you. We once said that was all that mattered."

"I never said I didn't love you. Why do you think this is so hard?"

He wrapped his arms around her and pulled her close to his chest. Gwen didn't put up a fight. When her head rested upon his hand, James nestled his face into the back of her neck and said, "We'll get through this. We've gotten through everything. Why would this be so different?"

He knew why. So did Gwen. His only hope was that his faulty bravado was enough to convince them that everything would be all right.

CHAPTER 7

GWEN

Gwen had no idea what she was thinking when she agreed to go out with James Sunday night. In her defense, though, she was under the impression they were going out for dinner and maybe taking in a show at the theater. Instead, James suggested that they dress for the club, and Gwen only knew of one club that they frequented.

Used to be she always had fun at The Dark Hour, the region's biggest and most exclusive club for men and women who had discerning sexual tastes. It was the type of place she instantly took to after starting to date James. After all, what humanized his fellow trust-fund kids better than showing them naked, drunk, and successfully hitting on every person in the room? (Perhaps other people would have found that daunting, but Gwen's personality lent her to becoming utterly delighted when Ian first hit on her, and James took it in stride.)

That was something she had always loved about James – his affable nature. The one that didn't take things too seriously, and the one that was always up for trying new things, even if he wasn't sure he'd like it.

Gwen didn't have much taste for The Dark Hour lately, though. What was once a fun biweekly escape had now become nothing but noise. She didn't recognize half the people there, even if they recognized her. When it came to her reputation preceding her, it usually had to do with kink.

Ah, there was the real reason she wasn't comfortable here anymore. It wasn't seeing other couples participate in their kinky natures. It was the expectation that she would indulge as well. Wasn't she the woman who once infamously cuckolded her own boyfriend for a whole night? The management liked to joke that it was couples like Gwen and James who kept the place buzzing and the money flowing. Too much pressure.

This was only their second time coming since Christmas. James probably thought he was grasping for familiarity. Gwen would rather go home and watch The Late Show reruns in bed. She had missed Wednesday's episode. Was it on again tonight?

"Gwenny," James said, leaning back in their leather sofa. Their corner of the club was cordoned off with a red velvet rope that only admitted the friends they wanted to talk to. So far, that was Kathryn and Ian, who canoodled on another couch while covertly watching YouTube videos on Ian's phone. (Phones were strictly not allowed in the club. Privacy concerns, after all.) "You're more uncomfortable than our frat brother Frank when he found out we were going to a pegging party five years ago. What's up?"

Gwen, who had been taking in the sights and raucous sounds of a sex club on a Sunday night, shrugged her shoulders and said, "Not really feeling it."

"What would help you feel it?"

His hand was on her thigh, fingers trudging up the skirt of her little black dress. "Maybe I want to sit here and watch the shows."

"We can watch the shows tonight." Nobody was scheduled to perform on the main stage that night, but that didn't stop amateurs from jumping up and arousing the crowds. James and Gwen used to be regulars and were *not* shy with the exhibitionism. Sometimes they joked that more people had seen Gwen naked than she had ever *been* naked in her life. *That feels like a lifetime ago.* In truth, it was about a year and a half ago when they last did something like that. Now, coming to the club meant looking into the eyes of everyone who judged them for what they went through with Cassandra. Didn't help that most of the men in the room had slept with Cassandra. Before the real paternity of little Patrick came to light, half the men in the city worried that they might be the daddy.

"Let's get a round of drinks," Ian said, pocketing his phone. Kathryn propped her elbow up on the back of their couch, her other hand drawing a small circle on the front of Ian's dress shirt. "Hell, let's get three rounds of drinks. We haven't played a drinking game in forever, and I'm itching for some fun around here."

"Nothing's stopping you two from getting frisky," James said.

"That's more your thing."

Gwen broke her brooding demeanor with a laugh. "Don't think we could ever top the night Kathryn ripped off your clothes, tied you up, and branded you with her lipstick."

Kathryn matched her friend's grin. "Yeah, hon, when are we gonna do that again?"

"Sounds like a wild bachelor party to me."

Ian was the only one laughing at his joke. Kathryn's smile crashed off her face, and James and Gwen were reminded of one of their biggest scars.

"Get those drinks," James said. "We'll play whatever game you want."

Gwen rolled her eyes as Ian flagged down a server and ordered three rounds of whatever shots the bar felt like giving them. "Can't wait to get drunk enough to stumble out of here."

"That's why we took a cab here, Gwen." Her partner patted her shoulder. The server bounded away, excited to be making such a good commission off two of the biggest couples in the club. "No worrying about getting home later."

The first round arrived on a circular tray. The server, who was busty enough to topple over when she set the tray down on the table, flashed everyone her most winning grin. Ian was the only one to flirt back with her.

"First round is the buzz." Ian handed his girlfriend a shot glass before grabbing one for himself. "Then we'll get serious."

James shoved a shot glass into Gwen's hand. With a sigh of resignation, she clinked her glass with her friends' and downed it in one gulp.

God, it burned!

"What *is* that?" She slammed her glass down on the table and gagged. "Demon piss?" Gwen used to be a professional bartender, yet she had *no* idea what she drank.

James clapped her on the back. She coughed as if that liquid threatened to shoot up her esophagus again. "Puts hair on your chest, doesn't it?"

"Puts *something* on my chest!"

Kathryn was the only one not falling over in grief when she put her empty shot glass down. Her prim and proper stance as she indulged in a drinking game was what separated her from Gwen, who flopped backward as if someone had punched her in the face and knocked her out. "Kinda woody, isn't it?"

"I know it killed my woody," Ian muttered.

"Give it five seconds. I'm sure you'll resurrect it."

Gwen felt the alcohol before anyone else did. Then again, her vision was so blurry, that everyone else could have thrown up their dinners and she would be none the wiser. "There's two more rounds of this shit coming?"

"God willing!"

The server returned with the second round. Ian was the first one up. Gwen was the last. *Not sure I can survive another one.* No matter how much she shook out her head, it felt impossible to down another shot of… whatever that was.

"Thought we were playing a game," James said. "God knows I need a reason to subject myself to this."

Ian sniffed the shot and almost put it back down again. Kathryn remained the only one completely nonplussed by the contents of her glass. "Before you take a drink," Ian said, glancing at his beloved in the sparkly white body-con dress, "you have to say what you love the most about your significant other."

"Now I *am* gonna gag," James said.

"I'll go first," Kathryn announced. To Ian, she said through pursed lips, "I love that you're not threatened by what a badass I am."

She downed her shot. Ian put a reassuring hand on her shoulder and with a curt nod, replied, "I'm very threatened. Every day, your badassery threatens to emasculate me, and for some reason I find that super-hot."

"Take the shot, Ian."

James laughed as his friend dumped the shot down his throat. Gwen slowly shook her head. *These two are almost as ridiculous as James and I used to be.*

Used to be. She hated admitting that.

"Your turn," Ian said, gesturing to James. "Tell us how much you love that Gwen isn't afraid to stick a dildo up your ass."

"That *was* on the tip of my tongue," James admitted. He grabbed Gwen's hand and picked up one of the remaining shot glasses. "Like this demon piss is about to be."

"Told you," Gwen said.

Her partner held the glass between their faces. "I love that she puts up with *allll* my bullshit." The dark blown liquid was soon out of the glass and in James's stomach.

"Can only imagine how much bullshit swims in your gut, James."

"*So* much!"

The alcohol was hitting everyone hard, and they hadn't drunk their third round. Gwen supposed it was time to join her friends in the revelry. Too bad she struggled to think of something to say.

Oh, there were many things she loved about James, but none of them were appropriate in the moment. The others had talked about what their lovers gave them, or put up with. It wasn't about *them,* specifically. *What is it about James that I love… and is something I don't expect from anyone else?*

Her partner swayed with a silly grin on his face. His expectant demeanor was enough to make Gwen snort in amusement. "I love that you understand all the reservations that I have."

James stopped smiling. Gwen hadn't spoken loudly enough for Kathryn and Ian to hear.

"Reservations, huh?"

Gwen continued to grin. Even after the disgusting drink was in her mouth, she smiled as if James should have absolutely understood what she said.

Before he could ask any questions, however, the third and final round of drinks arrived. After that, it was a free-for-all, because everyone was too tipsy and too battered by befouled drinks to think up a game to play.

The alcohol hit Gwen's head five minutes later. By then, it was too late to stop drinking, because the second and third drink she already imbibed was like a giant tank to the brain. She slumped against the couch. James had never looked so enticing.

Perhaps that had been part of the plan.

"Look at 'em, Gwenny." James brought her into his embrace while referencing the couple on the other couch. "Aren't they disgusting?"

Gwen couldn't think of the words to describe Kathryn hopping into her boyfriend's lap and making out with him like they were teenagers again. *Cute? Gross? Eye-roll-worthy?* Somehow, Gwen knew that a couple could be all three. "The worst," she finally said. "I'm gonna barf watching them."

James nipped her ear. His breath was ranker than what Gwen remembered from their shot glasses. "Maybe we should get some privacy and a little gross on our own."

"What was in that glass? Aphrodisiacs?"

"I really hope so."

Gwen put her hand on James's chest. "If you can stumble to the bathroom and pop a mint in your mouth, I *might* consider making out with you when you get back."

"What's this might business?"

"I know how you get when you're good and drunk. You think I want to have your mouth on mine when you fall asleep?"

"I didn't used to be that bad…"

"We're older, James."

"Indeed." With a sigh, James sat up, wobbling from how the alcohol suddenly hit him. "Guess that means I really should go to the bathroom, then. Getting older, you know."

"Empty the hose, and we'll talk."

"Yes, ma'am." James pushed himself off the couch. Gwen had to admire how well he kept it together on his way to the men's room. "I'll bring back two condoms!" he called over his shoulder. "One for both sides!"

Ian came up for air amid his hot and heavy make-out session with Kathryn. "*Please* tell me that means what I think it means?"

"Why?" Kathryn grabbed him by the chin and turned his mouth back to hers. "You interested in trying something fun and new tonight, honey?"

Growling, Ian shoved Kathryn backward onto the couch, practically on top of her by the time her giggles finished peppering the air. "I love you when you're drunk."

"And I love you when you're drunk! Let's get married!"

Gwen rolled her eyes. The only time anyone heard those words come out of Kathryn's mouth was when she was full of liquor. Why did she have a feeling that sometimes bit her friend in the ass?

Five minutes later, James rounded the corner, suddenly sober.

"It's Patrick," he said, face white and hand clenching his phone.

His friends sat up. Gwen's eyes widened. "What happened?" everyone asked.

James handed Gwen his phone. "I got a call from Cassandra. Apparently, they're all at the hospital because he has a high fever."

"You better go," Ian said.

James looked to his partner, who attempted to shake off the effects of alcohol as she grabbed her purse. "What hospital," she asked, sure that she sounded like a bigger mess than she really felt.

"St. John's."

"Of course. Can't go anywhere but St. John's." She put her hand on James's arm, both to steady herself, and to – hopefully – reassure him. "He'll be fine. Let's go."

"You're going with me?"

Their hands were intertwined. "Yes," Gwen said with finality.

She was too tipsy to understand what she had really agreed to, but by then, they were already on their way to the nearest hospital.

***

It wasn't difficult to find the Welshes in the private wing of St. John's Hospital. They were the small family still dressed in their Armani and Chanel, as if that's what they wore to bed every night.

James almost shoved aside the poor nurse leading him and Gwen when he caught sight of Cassandra from the other end of the waiting room. The delicate debutante sat up, her face reddened with tears and fright. Her mother's hand rubbed her back, and her father's eyes remained fixed on James.

The gang was all here. The only thing shocking Gwen was that they hadn't brought the nanny and an assistant along.

No, wait. *There* was the nanny, coming out of the restroom to find the Welshes and the Meranges clashing together in the middle of an otherwise quiet waiting room.

"James!" Cassandra leaped up from her seat and went straight to him. Good thing Gwen hadn't decided to get in the way. Otherwise, she would soon find herself against the wall or on the floor. *Bad enough I want to be there, anyway.* The alcohol had not worn off as quickly for her. Anxiety had been efficient at rousing James's survival instincts, but Gwen was still stumbling against the furniture and really, really cursing Ian Mathers for ordering three rounds of shots. *For a former bartender, I sure don't hold my liquor well.*

"Cassie." James embraced her. Gwen was going to be sick, and the alcohol was not helping that conundrum. "How's Patrick? What happened?"

"He… I don't know… he just… wasn't well all of a sudden, and when I took his temperature…"

Sarah Welsh approached them with the haughty demeanor of a woman who knew better than anyone else in the room. That included the nurse at her station, and the doctor shuffling down the hall to check on a different baby in the NICU. "Patrick had a bit of a fever, and we thought it best to bring him into the hospital for a checkup. I'm sure everything will be fine." She rubbed James's arm with a smile, as if *he* were her son-in-law. Gwen, meanwhile, stayed far out of everyone's way. She didn't want them smelling the alcohol on her breath.

"What if I… what I got him sick…" Cassandra clasped her hands over her face and flung herself into James's arms. Nah. Gwen was definitely going to be the sick one if she didn't get her ass to the women's room in thirty seconds.

She attempted to wash the club and the alcohol off her body. Luckily, she carried a travel toothbrush set in her purse, and by the time she gave her teeth a good scrub and re-emerged from the bathroom, everyone had settled back down into the waiting room. Mr. Welsh fell asleep on the end of his couch while the nanny texted on her phone. Sarah and James flanked Cassandra on another couch, assuring her that she wasn't a terrible mother and that babies got sick all the time. Yes, even the babies that grew up in the lap of luxury.

She really loves that boy, I guess. Gwen knew that already, but seeing the tragically beautiful Cassandra Welsh sobbing over her child put some perspective into the hearts around her. *I can't fault her for that.* Gwen could, however, fault the young mother for dragging James into this shitfest. If the boy wasn't in danger of dying, did it really require his father to be there? A phone call in the morning should have been sufficient.

Not that Gwen was jealous or anything.

The doctor emerged ten minutes later with good news: Patrick had the flu, but to be on the safe side, he would like to keep the boy for the night to make sure he was hydrated.

"Things like these are so hard to prevent no matter how you slice it," the genial doctor said to the group in the waiting room. "Patrick didn't have his flu shot this winter, did he?"

"His pediatrician worried that he might be immunocompromised," Sarah explained.

"That could do it. More than likely either yourselves or members of your staff brought it into the home. Boys Patrick's age are quite susceptible to…"

Sarah interrupted him. "*Everyone* is required to have their shots before they work in my home. My husband has health issues of his own, and since Patrick was born, I've been extra diligent about making sure everyone…" she turned to Irene, still texting. "Wait. Did *you* have your flu shot this year?"

"Uh…" The nanny looked up from her phone. "I… think so? I had some kind of shot before Christmas, Madam Welsh."

"I knew it," Sarah snapped. "That man you go gallivanting off to see on Tuesdays. He's probably *riddled* with diseases."

James intervened before the nanny could be embarrassed in the middle of a hospital waiting room. "It could've as easily been me." Never mind Gwen knew for a fact that both she and James had their flu shots… it had been made *very clear* to them that nobody was visiting Patrick until needles were in arms. James had quipped that it might prevent him from getting the flu that year. Who knew!

"James…" Cassandra put her hands on his.

"Anyway," the doctor motioned to a door at the end of the short hallway. "Now's a good time to see him, Mr. and Mrs. Merange."

Nobody corrected him. Not even Gwen, who swallowed a lump the size of her oncoming headache down her throat. James shared one exasperated look at her as he stood up, Cassandra's hand still in his. The look was apologetic, but Gwen knew what it meant. "*Sorry, hon. I've gotta do this. Be right back.*"

Gwen didn't bother closing the gap between herself and the Welshes. They likewise did not acknowledge her.

Nobody was forbidden from going up to the Patrick's room door and stealing a peek. Gwen had no intention of doing that. It wasn't her business. Plenty of people could line up in front of her to see her stepson.

She sat down on a chair on the far side of the room. Fifteen minutes later, she nearly fell asleep.

Suppose it wouldn't hurt to go get a countdown to when we can go home…

She didn't look at the Welshes as she tiptoed down the hall – well, *flailed* down the hall, because getting up on her heels after three shots of liquor and fatigue claiming her did not lend itself to tiptoeing – and quietly approached Patrick's door. Gwen didn't know what she expected to behold. A toddler sleeping in a hospital bed made for children his size. His parents quietly discussing what to do now that their son had survived his first real hospitalization since his birth.

Instead, Gwen saw something she was never meant to see.

Both James and Cassandra stood over their son's bed, silent and full of their private thoughts Gwen would never understand. Cassandra sniffed every few seconds, her red eyes and the tear stains on her cheeks begging someone to take pity on her. The infuriating part? Gwen genuinely did not believe Ms. Welsh did that on purpose. She was so absorbed in the well-being of her little boy that there was no space in her heart or head to seduce everyone into taking care of *her.*

That's how she was. Gwen would never understand what it was like to be Cassandra. Cassandra probably barely understood it.

So why was Gwen so surprised to see James wrap his arm around the mother of his child and accept a sob to his chest.

No, it wasn't the act that surprised her. James was such an empathetic dumbass that he would pick a crying woman off the street and give her a big hug and a wad of cash. That was supposed to be *endearing* about him. James shirking the mother of his own child, and the girl he once called his best friend, would have been more shocking.

What sliced Gwen open at the gut, however, was how perfect they looked together.

Was there a couple in town that looked more beautiful and natural than James Merange and Cassandra Welsh? No wonder everyone around them thought they would get married.

No wonder people looked at Gwen with shock and disbelief. It wasn't her pedestrian background that made people reel. It was the fact she wasn't Cassandra – not even a little bit, not even in the hair, the face, or the demeanor. James's destiny had marked him as a fated match for a demure woman like Cassandra. The perfect foil to his outgoing yet lovable personality.

Gwen could easily see them as The Meranges, that well-welcomed union of two old families that were always meant to merge. The chuckles about Sarah and Albert would come full circle as their children married and accomplished what they never could in the eyes of the public. James would be the hardworking businessman as he prepared to take over his family's company and continue to make millions of dollars a week. Cassandra would be the quiet socialite who heralded pet causes and raised her black-haired children to be as kind as their father and as sophisticated as her. How many kids could they have? Three? Four? James had the fortitude to take on a big brood, and Cassandra seemed the type to define herself by her family. The yearly family portraits would be the talk of the country club.

Where could Gwen possibly fit into that? She didn't have that kind of bond with James. Nor did she look at children with the sort of gaze James begat his son.

I don't want to see this… The reason Gwen had foregone visiting Patrick didn't have much to do with how uncomfortable the Welshes made her, and everything to do with James's destiny to be a dad one day. *Where does that leave me?*

Gwen put her hand on her stomach and pretended she didn't have flashbacks to two years ago.

"Please don't be sick outside of my grandson's room." Sarah Welsh approached from behind, keeping her voice down. "He already has the flu. He doesn't need whatever you have."

Gwen whipped her head around, ire burning from her throat to her eyes. "Trust me. I don't want much to do with this."

"Good Lord." Sarah looked as if Gwen had doused herself in vinegar. "Are you drunk? You reek of liquor."

"Didn't drink any less than James."

"I'll pretend that was in English, and inform you that because your man can drink half the alcohol in the room and still stand up, doesn't mean that it's becoming of a lady." Sarah sniffed, gazing into the room. "Not that I expect you to know much about being a lady."

"You're right. I don't. I didn't go to those fancy boarding and finishing schools."

"Just the school of hard knocks, right?" That wasn't true humor in Sarah's voice, even though she chuckled. "It's none of my business who the father of my grandchild cavorts with. He's not married to my daughter, after all." The way she gazed into the room dictated that she wouldn't mind the idea, though. "But I will warn you that I will not tolerate any of this…" Sarah flicked her finger in Gwen's direction, "around my young and impressionable grandson. I hold everyone who comes around him to a high standard."

"Don't worry about me." Gwen turned away from the door before she was truly sick. "I have no intention of butting into your grandson's life."

"Curious how you'll manage that, when James inevitably asks for visitation rights as the boy gets older."

Gwen didn't say anything.

"Or do you not plan on being around long enough for that to happen?"

There were a million words swimming in the back of Gwen's head, but she knew none of them were good enough to speak her mind while putting Madam Welsh in her place. This woman was worse than a mother-in-law. She was a master manipulator. Were people like her even truly capable of love? Did she really love her daughter? Did she really love Albert? Or were they mere pawns to make her feel better, to give her a place in the world?

Where did James fall into Madam Welsh's plan?

Gwen knew where she fell. Nowhere. If anything, Gwen was a hindrance to the master plan Sarah Welsh had concocted the moment she gave birth to a girl and her lover begat a boy.

It didn't help that when Gwen glanced back in that room, she was met with every reason James should be with Cassandra instead of her.

SEVEN YEARS AGO

Part 2

Gwen emerged from the back room of the bar to find James there, *again.*

She shook her head in nothing but curious amusement. That guy showed up twice or thrice a week at the most awkward time. (Was it too much to ask to have no customers while Gwen cleaned up and prepped for the rush sure to come in the next two hours?) Usually, he kept to himself, but occasionally he made light conversation with her. That didn't count the amount of times she glanced over her shoulder while she did some dishes or took inventory and caught him staring at her ass.

Typical. Men always stared at her ass. They often hit on her, too. It wasn't a Saturday night unless Gwen made a pile of tips because she charmed the men that came into the bar into thinking they had even the slightest bit of a chance with her.

Okay, so sometimes they did. Gwen didn't make a habit of it, but for the right guy, she was willing to go home and have a good time. Bonus points if he came into the bar again *and* continued to give her tips. As long as they didn't think she was their girlfriend, all was good.

James was trouble.

Cute, charming trouble.

Their conversations over the past few weeks had revealed that he was in training to take over his family's business, whatever it was. Once guys started talking about *business,* Gwen tuned them out. Blah, blah, blah. Stocks, bonds, buyouts, and mergers. Whatever. Sounded like a goofy '80s movie.

James was a goofy kind of guy. He may have looked like he stepped out of a men's watch catalog – that wasn't knocking his appearance, by the way – and was affable enough to joke around with, but every time James started saying something serious, he pulled back and turned it into a jest instead.

At least he was genuinely funny, and he didn't rely on crass, offensive humor to get his points across. While most of those jokes weren't fit for a kid's ear, Gwen didn't have to hear curse word after slur, and that was always a pleasant night at the bar.

That night, when she emerged to find her favorite customer waiting for her at the far end of the bar, she spared him a smile and approached with a slight wave of her hand. "Hey, stranger," she said. "Get you the usual?"

"If the usual will make me forget that meeting I had earlier."

Gwen had a feeling it would, especially if she pumped it with a little extra liquor. "Bad day at the office again?"

"The *worst.* My dad is a tyrant. News at eleven."

Chuckling, Gwen swiftly made his favorite drink using the same top shelf stuff he singlehandedly made them reorder more than once since he started coming around. "Your life is so hard. Mr. Trust Fund."

"Hey, I work for that trust fund." James winked at her when the glass appeared before him. "I work to keep my father happy. A happy father means a happy trust fund for many years to come."

"Is that how they work? I wouldn't know. I'm from scholarship country." Gwen braced herself against the bar. She knew her breasts were pushed toward James's face, but she had long since decided she didn't care if he respectfully ogled her. The man paid her enough tips to make her think she was in one of *those* clubs, anyway. Might as well give him a little extra for his time.

"Of course it's not how they work. But if I pretend it is, I can feel like I have more control over my fate."

"Ah, yes, fate. Is that what keeps bringing you into my bar?"

"Why, Ms. Mitchell," James said with a waggle of his eyebrows, "are you finally flirting back with me in earnest?"

She snorted. "You'd like that, I bet."

"I mean, your lovely face and ability to banter with me is the second reason I keep coming back here."

"Only the second?"

"The drinks are top notch, Gwen. I'm telling you, it's amazing this place doesn't have more customers."

She laughed. "Wanna hear a secret? I don't water your drinks down."

She left him with that nugget as she walked away. She would have been disappointed if he weren't staring at her ass.

James was the kind of customer Gwen appreciated while always keeping a careful eye on him. Guys like that? The ones with the big wallets and not afraid to drop in during the slow times to make light conversation and crack jokes? They usually wanted something. Namely, *her*.

Gwen had been dealing with guys like James for years, long before she started bartending full time. Apparently, she had a cool *je ne sais quoi* that made her popular with men of all types and backgrounds. Most of them weren't worth her time. Occasionally, she picked up a temporary boyfriend or a one-night stand that was adequate enough for her to keep doing it. But there were some men that made her uneasy, and she wasn't sure why.

Sure, creeps were creeps, and Gwen smelled them from a mile away. Those were the obvious ones. Sometimes guys were so good at hiding their creep levels that Gwen went out on dates and soon regretted it. After a few years of dealing with one creep after another, she was content to live the single life and ignore any guy who followed established patterns of behavior.

She couldn't make out what kind of guy James Merange was.

Lovable buffoon that had a crush on her? Or a sinister playboy playing the long con? Some unholy mix of the two?

Gwen returned to the counter to find James glancing at her from his phone. Did he think she was fooling her with the old, *I'm on my phone* trick? The screen was black.

She was curious enough to ask him what his deal was, but knew better than to risk whatever professional bartender-client relationship they maintained. No matter how cute James was, Gwen was better off…

"Do you have a boyfriend, Gwen?"

Ah. There it was. His next move would be to hit on her.

A part of Gwen wanted to see where it went. It had nothing to do with his supposed money, either. (Gwen didn't bother Googling him or his family until they started going out. What an eye opener *that* was…) James was intriguing, wasn't he? Boyish charms encased in a mature, masculine air. A youthful quality that clashed against his expensive clothes and a smart head for business. James wasn't childlike or immature. He was in careful control of his humor. For all Gwen knew, these trips to the bar were one of his only chances to let his real nature shine. *That almost makes me feel special.* He chose to be around her when letting off steam. Alone, but was he really alone when Gwen was only a shout away? They had casual conversations for weeks before taking it further.

Casual enough for him to ask if she had a boyfriend? Maybe.

"I'm single," Gwen said, standing a few feet more than usual away from him. Survival instinct. James would either take the news graciously, or he would up the sleaze. As much as Gwen wanted to believe that James was different… she wouldn't be surprised if he wasn't. Life had jaded her.

James narrowed his eyes, sat back, and asked, "How?"

Crossing his arms was a nice touch, but Gwen wasn't buying it. "What do you mean *how?* How what? Do I not have a boyfriend?"

"Yes. Unless you broke up with someone five hours ago, I'm not sure how you could possibly be single."

"Like I haven't heard this pickup line before."

"Who says I'm trying to pick you up? I'm trying to understand how someone as nice and amiable as you is *single.*"

She snorted. "Not all of us want to be attached to the old ball and chain."

"Who said anything about marriage? I'm talking about having a man who treats you right and puts that extra skip in your step."

"And is easy on the eyes, I'm sure."

James grinned. *Damnit. That's the kind of grin that gets girls in trouble.* Not Gwen, though. She had sworn off getting in trouble. "Let me know if you do find a guy like that. Maybe I'd like to date him."

Gwen paled. Oh, no. She had never considered that after all this time…

James might be *gay!*

"What?" He pocketed his phone and pointed to the exasperated look on Gwen's face. "Got a problem with a guy who's comfortable with who he is?"

"Not at all." Woo, boy. Gwen's best friend from high school, now going by the drag queen name of *Lady Priss-zilla,* would love to hear that she had offended a gay guy. "Just didn't think you were… never mind. You want me to top that drink off for you?"

James didn't directly answer the question. Not that one, anyway. Instead, he tugged on his growing facial hair and with a wag of the eyebrows said, "I'll have you know that I have much more experience with the ladies."

"Uh huh."

"Just… what happens in Texas, stays in Texas."

"Texas?"

"Long story. There was this conference, some guy from Montreal with a hot French accent… bah. Loose lips sink ships."

"Maybe I should be asking if *you* have a boyfriend, James."

"Why?" Her perked up. "You interested? Because I could tell Ronaldo to pack his stuff and be out of my condo by midnight."

"A French Canadian named Ronaldo? Send him to my house instead."

"At least we've established that you like guys."

"We've established the same thing about you!" Gwen leaned against the counter and crossed her arms. "Are you hitting on me or not? I can't tell anymore."

"*How* could you misconstrue this as anything but intense flirting to get you more intimately into my life, Gwen?"

"You started talking about some guy named Ronaldo."

"You're confused. He doesn't exist." James continued to grin. "Unlike you."

"You're right. I do exist. As I'm sure you've established over these past few weeks you've come in here to make eyes at me."

Chuckling, James leaned forward again and said, "So you've noticed?"

"A guy going out of his way to come in here during my off-hours? Getting to know me through trite conversation?" Gwen met him halfway across the counter, her grin grand enough to suck him into a deadly vortex of her making. *Think I'll let him live, though. Why not? Could be fun.* James wasn't pinging any warning bells. The worst he'd do was get over Gwen the moment she gave in to him. She'd miss the tips, but…

Maybe it was worth it for the thrill?

"Yeah, I've noticed," Gwen continued. "Kinda hard to miss in a boring place like this."

"So you're saying I'm *not* boring?"

She laughed. "Are you always this self-deprecating? Because it's kinda cute."

"I can be the most self-critical prick you've ever met if it means making you smile."

Didn't she give him the reaction he wanted? Gwen could hardly contain the giddiness surfacing in her chest, and when she laughed again, it was with a hearty guffaw that almost made James join her in such madness.

"Damn," he said, "does this mean if I don't ask you out right now, I'll lose my chance forever?"

"Why forever?"

He cocked his head. "I might not have the guts to try again."

"Oh, now I don't believe that." Yet Gwen swelled with the knowledge that she had the power to fell this man's ego with a simple "no." She wasn't a whim. She wasn't someone he thought he might have a chance with, so why not ask? Almost like he fancied her so much that he subjected himself to this thrice-weekly charade of being a simple customer in a lonely, mid-tier bar. More customers would show up later and dominate Gwen's time. James needed to take his chance now if he were going to tonight. "You mean guys don't do those endless pursuits like I see in the movies?"

"I'm told that's creepy, so I've cut back on it."

"You don't wanna be creepy?"

"Can't say it's in my nature. Catch more flies with honey, right?"

He finished his drink, smacking his lips when the glass touched the counter. His large breaths made his chest contract against his fitted dress shirt. Gwen had to refrain from biting her bottom lip as she openly checked out James in his work clothes. *He smells like a million dollars. Can you even buy his cologne in department stores?* Probably not. His cologne was purchased in an ivory New York tower, where one required a membership to enter, and memberships were only handed out to princely sons and their spoiled sisters.

Gwen glanced at the clock. She could have this place closed now and reopened later without anyone – least of all her boss – finding out.

***

Cleaning supplies fell off the nearby desk when Gwen was slammed against the wall. "No, no!" she said, pushing James off her and taking his hand. "*This* corner. The security camera looks right over here!"

He was too flushed with disbelief that this was happening to mind his words. "Maybe I'm cool with a little exhibition. Can be fun in the right moment."

Giggling, Gwen drew him into a cramped, dark corner of the office. "This isn't the right moment for that."

"Aw, it's not?"

She cupped his scruffy cheeks between her hands, desperation mounting in the pit of her warm stomach. "Maybe some other time."

"You've already decided that there's going to be another time?"

Gwen pulled him into her arms. It took two seconds for her to confidently hop up and wrap her legs around his waist. *Ah, there it is. The crazy need to fuck a guy.* When she made the decision to let him into the back room for a little romp, she wasn't sure if she wanted to be wooed or *dominated.* Well, maybe not dominated. This wasn't some naughty erotic romance novel, after all. Even if James were wealthy enough to be named Christian Grey and she… well, she was no Anastasia "The Virgin" Steele. No casting director wouldn't look twice at her when lining up that list of characters. But she was the blue-collar heroine looking for a little fun, a little heat, and a whole lotta adventure. James could provide some of that, if only for a night.

Their first kiss was both tentative and intense. The kind of first kiss that left a permanent imprint on her mind. Even if she never saw James again, that single kiss held the power to make her pine for him every night for the rest of her life. Other men could come and go. She could marry some perfectly nice boy and live a comfortable life. But she would never, ever forget the kiss she stole in the office in the back of the bar. Not when the man smelled like the billions in his trust fund and slammed her against the wall like a fiend.

A gasp eked from her lips when James pushed her up the wall, his face in her breasts and her hands wrapping tightly around the back of his neck.

"How long have you been waiting for this, huh?" Gwen asked.

Her shirt ascended her torso. The plaid overshirt on her arms was soon on the floor. Even the t-shirt covering her sports bra was too much clothing for a man in a three-piece suit. "Since the first night I saw you in this bar," James confessed.

That was one of the corniest things he could say, but Gwen wasn't going to deny that she wanted to hear more corny words from James Merange. Somehow, he made them earnest. There was something about him that was inherently trustworthy. Not just for a playmate in the bedroom. For a future husband, if Gwen could ever believe it.

No way. I'm getting waaay ahead of myself!

"To be fair," she said, his kisses on her bare stomach driving her mad, "I've been into you since you first walked into my bar, too."

He slammed his mouth against hers. "I know," he muttered.

Gwen didn't usually do this, but when the moment called for having a quickie with a relative stranger in the back office of her place of employment… she wasn't going to ignore her instincts. They had been good to her for most of her life. When her body whispered, "*Go ahead and have some fun with him,*" she was inclined to listen.

And enjoy herself.

While Gwen was familiar with men and their diverse bodies and ways of making love, she was still surprised to discover how different James was. It wasn't only the tantalizing scent of his cologne and the natural odor beneath his clothes. Nor was it limited to the powerful kisses devouring her lips and the strong hands feeling up her shirt and squeezing her breasts. It was the breadth of his chest, the bite of his tongue, and the quiet grunts of disbelief that he could be with a woman like *her*. Gwen didn't feel like she was "giving in" to him. Nor was she indulging him. This was purely about their mutual attraction and fate dictating who she went out with for a while.

Maybe this wasn't forever, but it wasn't just a night, either. Gwen knew that the moment James groaned into her mouth and finished unzipping her jeans.

"Hold up, big boy," she said with a grin against his cheek. "You better not be…"

She slid down the wall so he could rummage through his pockets. The urgency of his actions was almost adorable. *He's so eager to fuck me that he's going to take twice as long looking through his belongings than if he calmed the hell down.* She wanted to laugh, but that risked hurting his feelings. Gwen didn't want that kind of negativity in the room. She wanted nothing but mirth and raw, sexual potency to guide her through these next five minutes.

"Oh, thank God." James let out a sigh of relief when he finally found his wallet. Not because he cared about the cash and credit cards, but because he had a condom in there, and *that* was the most important thing in the world. "I was going to feel like a stupid jackass."

"Aw." Gwen welcomed him back into her arms. "You could still be a stupid jackass. Live your dreams."

"My dreams include fucking you, if that's okay."

"Am I sending mixed signals or something? The only thing stopping you right now is your stamina."

"I've got *plenty* of stamina."

Gwen grinned. "Prove it."

Oh, he did.

They went for the proverbial quickie not only because Gwen had a limited amount of time before customers started showing up to the bar, but because it was *hot.* The rush, the urgency, the incredible need for one another that they shared was enough to fell lesser humans, but Gwen and James embraced it as if they had nothing else to gain from this one-off tryst that could easily span the rest of their lives.

"Wow. You're... wow."

Gwen was too aroused to chastise James for his lack of a vocabulary. Not when those were his fingers slipping inside of her and marveling at how wet she already was. *Okay, maybe I had a head start because he's so good looking.* Having him slam her against the wall and go at her like a beast? Yeah, she was a little wet. Just a little.

James was pretty *wow* himself. All he showed her was the top few buttons of his shirt undone... and his cock.

She wanted to say something smart, something he would remember for the rest of his life every time he looked down and saw his cock in his hand. Yet Gwen was at a loss for words once she realized that this was happening. She was being a bad girl at work, and James was the bad boy she had chosen for a wild adventure.

So, maybe she wouldn't use her words. Maybe she'd let her body do all the talking. Not like she was going anywhere with him pressed between her legs like that!

"Oh, *hell* yes!" Gwen cried when he slowly entered her, his breaths echoing in the small corner of the office, and her voice a stark reminder that what they were doing was *naughty. If he wants naughty, I can give him naughty.* Was it naughty to have a body that greedily welcomed him, even if their descent into sexual madness was ripe with friction and what came with discovering each other's physical quirks for the first time? (Yes.) The moment James was all the way in, his breath consuming the soft flesh of her throat and his hands clenching her thighs, Gwen swore that this was meant to be.

All the way down to how he kissed her as he began to thrust.

Years later, when they had ample time to reflect upon the long, languid road of their relationship, Gwen would safely say that their first time having sex was "*Perfect.*" Someone watching them, however, may have begged to differ. Was it really perfect if she had to stop and ask him to readjust himself so he didn't quite dig so *much* into the wrong corner of her pussy? How could it be perfect if he bruised her thighs because he didn't think about how much strength he used to hold her up? Or what the hell was so perfect about the awkward sound coming out of Gwen's mouth when James hit her favorite spot halfway through fucking her? She sounded like a mangled duck, for fuck's sake! It was a miracle he didn't pull out and ask if she were the Ugly Duckling instead of a swan princess!

But those were the little quirks of a first time – of every time – that made it perfect. Memorable. A fun story for Gwen to tell the girls for years to come. She would smile every time she recalled James saying, "*Hang on, my hip is cramping,*" as if his cramping hip was comparable to the strain put on her tailbone as it continued to slide down the wall every time he thrust into her core. Both showed their humanity in the span of five glorious minutes. The fact it felt good and sated their sexual curiosities was a bonus.

How could it be any more perfect than that?

Gwen clung to his broad shoulders when she sensed he was on the verge of climaxing. The sort of elation infiltrating her body wasn't necessarily orgasmic – in fact, she would never remember if she properly climaxed or not that night – but it was the type of pleasure akin to cruising down the beachside highway on a sunny day, the top down and the warm breeze whipping in her hair. It was a rush. It claimed her like he claimed her, one powerful movement of his hips at a time.

Her fingers dug into his suit. Wrinkled it beyond repair.

There was something quietly infectious about the way their tryst concluded. James blushed when Gwen's feet touched the ground and she threaded her fingers through her tousled hair. The boyish way he fixed his own hair and offered to smooth down the errant strand of blond sticking up on her head made her shudder. Not even having sex had made her shudder like that.

That was beyond intimate. Had they been in bed, Gwen would have easily thrown her arm across his chest and snuggled into the crook of his neck. The endorphins fueling her thoughts needed an outlet. How fair was it to stand there with nothing to say but, "Thanks?"

James lightly kissed her forehead. "I've gotta… uh…" Was he still blushing? Why? Wasn't he Mr. Confident?

"Bathroom's right through there." Gwen pointed. "Hurry up, though. It's the only one we've got, and I've gotta use it too." Someone needed to wash up before going back to work.

"Maybe you should go first." Except for that thing neither of them mentioned. Gwen wasn't about to suggest that her lover throw out the condom in the trashcan. She had *some* decorum.

"Oh, give me that." She wasn't shy, particularly about her own bodily fluids. She had to wash her hands anyway, right? Might as well take on the role of utmost responsibility and ditch the condom deep in the pits of the bathroom trash. *I have to take it out at the end of my shift, anyway!*

Gwen didn't expect to see James when she came out of the bathroom ten minutes later. But there he was, milling about the bar in his wrinkled suit yet still looking like the son of a million dollars.

There were two patrons in the bar, looking around for their bartender. When they saw Gwen's face, their own lit up. James disappeared into the bathroom, and Gwen got back to work.

Well, that was fun. She could only chuckle to herself as she made two martinis and served the two women sitting at the bar. They continued to gab about their night class at the local community college and how it conflicted with their ability to pick up their kids after school. Something about Kaylynn's soccer practice and Bradlynn's choir group. Gwen was too infatuated with what had happened in the back room to care what these two women had to say.

That was good sex, right? Gwen pretended to study the bottles on the top shelf, as if she were deciding which to replace and which to measure. Nobody would know she reflected upon the quickie she shared with James behind that wall. *His kisses were definitely the best… but I wonder how he would be in an actual bed…*

James rapped on the bar, startling her. Gwen spun around. There he was, the man of her hour, looking like he was stepping out for work.

"I've gotta get going," he said. "See you next time?"

"You're coming back?"

His pleasant smile faltered. "Am I not welcomed back?"

The women at the other end of the bar had stopped talking and stared at them. Gwen brushed them off with a sigh and said, "See you next time, James."

He hesitated before leaving, a friendly wave the only thing left in his wake. Gwen peered after him before resolving to get back to work. She could reflect upon making love to James Merange later.

"Your boyfriend?" one of the women asked. "He's cute."

Gwen flipped the switch that transformed her into the amiable bartender, ready to fish for tips and pour drinks. Maybe in that order. "I guess so. He's a friend, anyway."

"Ah, look at you blush!" said the other woman. "Reminds me of when I was your age."

"You seriously can't be that much older than me."

"Not really! I got married early and started having kids right away. But it feels like a lifetime ago." The woman elbowed her friend. "Think Joe would mind if I took off with that guy who left just now? Oh, sorry," she said to Gwen. "Don't mean to make you think I'm going after your boyfriend."

"He's not my…"

"Gwen!" James was back, slapping his hands on the bar top and startling her once more. "When's your next day off?"

She looked at him as if he had sprouted a second head. "Tuesday?"

"Tues… drat." He put his hands on his hips. "All right. Tell you what. Promise me a date on Tuesday, and I'll cancel all my business plans. We'll do whatever you want. How about the planetarium? You wanna go to the planetarium?"

Was that the first thing he thought of? Adorable. "Never been to the planetarium. Is it even open on Tuesdays?"

"If it's not, I'll make them open it. We'll have it all to ourselves."

His earnest manner beguiled her. "All right, James. You and me. The planetarium on Tuesday."

"Awesome. See you there." He had an extra skip to his step as he walked out. The women teased Gwen for daring to decry that man as her boyfriend.

Five minutes later, James came running back in.

"Your number!" Gwen had been pouring a new patron his drink. "I need your number!"

She told him he could have it if they ever went on a second date.

Seven years later, her number had yet to change, and James could recite it off the top of his head.

CHAPTER 8

JAMES

Patrick's health scare had been enough to send James to his doctor later that week. He had an hour to spare between a business lunch and a gathering with his peers at a local lounge. Plenty of time for his doctor to draw some blood and take his usual vitals.

And ask a slew of invasive questions.

Doubtlessly this doctor, who was known for being one of the best for anyone with means, had heard the rumors that James's son had not been conceived via conventional means. Yet James had never suggested otherwise. Which was why he wasn't surprised when the doctor started asking after his sexual health as if he planned on having more kids anytime soon.

The doctor's job wasn't to judge, after all. He could easily assume that James was knocking up Cassandra every two years. He could also follow that up with, "So how's Gwen?"

James rolled down his sleeves while the doctor washed his hands in the nearby sink. "Gorgeous and not taking any flak from anyone. Least of all me."

Chuckles overpowered the flow of water from the tap. "Sounds like the perfect woman. I'll be sure to share that sentiment with my wife later." The sink turned off. The doctor turned around, paper towel in his hand. "Is she doing okay since the, uh…"

That could've meant a number of things, but James had a good feeling this wasn't about the surprise stepson Gwen received one day. "She's doing great. Keep trying to convince her that we should go on a trip soon. Get out of town, you know. It's been a dire winter with all the damned snow and dreariness of… well, you know."

"Indeed, I do." The doctor crossed his arms. "Did you follow my recommendation for a relationship counselor?"

"Ah, no…" James rubbed the back of his neck. "I brought it up, but she wasn't into it."

"It's true that it doesn't work that well unless you both want it. Yet the counselor I referred you to is one of the best in the state. Can't go wrong with her."

"Does that mean she has a 100% success rate?"

"Nobody does," the doctor said with a laugh. "You're a businessman. You know how true that is."

James sighed. "Thanks. I'll try bringing it up again."

"Tell her that there are a lot of new treatments these days that can help a woman in her position."

"*Thanks.*" James hoped the doctor would leave it there. He meant well, but he never heard what Gwen said late at night, when she had one too much to drink and looked at her partner's cock as if it were a free-for-all buffet. *One week since I knew such loveliness.* Still didn't compare to how it used to be.

James texted Cassandra on his way out of the doctor's office. She confirmed that their son – who had been back home for a few days – was almost finished with his flu, and James was more than welcome to come visit whenever was good for him.

He checked his watch before replying, *"I'd rather talk to you, if it's all right. Can you meet me downtown in fifteen minutes?"*

***

As much as James yearned to see his son, he was relieved that Cassandra didn't have time to get Patrick ready for a brief excursion into the city. She arrived at the lounge five minutes later than James had asked to see her, apologies spilling from her lips.

"No need to apologize." He remained seated while the lounge host pulled out a chair for Cassandra. When she sat, her bag strap slipped off her shoulder and plummeted into her lap. Her penchant for form-fitting yet conservative dresses reminded James of women like Monica Warren and Kathryn Alison, two very well-to-do ladies who exuded the type of class and sophistication the social elite commended. Too bad Cassandra had lost her chance at that level of notoriety. She was always the type to be more *infamous* than anything else.

Cassandra shook her head, the rose-shaped barrette in her black hair coming loose. She didn't seem to notice it. "I swear I started getting ready the moment you asked me to meet you. But my mother caught me on the way out the door, and…" she stopped. "You don't want to hear my excuses. I'm sure you'd much rather talk about Patrick."

"He was on my mind, yes." James fingered the top of his glass, in which his favorite brand of whisky – on the rocks, of course – settled. He had ordered it because he figured he might need a little liquid courage to get through this meeting, but found that he wasn't that interested in imbibing so early in the day. *I'll have drinks with the guys later… is this really what I want to be doing right now?* Yes. No. Maybe?

"You'll be relieved to know that he's back to his old self already. The doctor says he's not contagious or anything." Cassandra ordered a cosmopolitan from the waitress approaching their corner table. As soon as the soft words were off her lips, the waitress exited the small chamber, pulling back a curtain behind her. James had taken extra precautions to make sure nobody knew they were meeting. Not because he was ashamed of being seen with his old friend and the mother of his child, but because the rumor mill was always experiencing a high season. *I don't need the whole world gabbing that I'm leaving Gwen. Again.*

"I am relieved to hear that he's doing better." James met her lingering gaze and looked away. "I was worried about him. So was Gwen."

Cassandra's shoulders stiffened at the sound of Gwen's name. "How is she doing?"

Angry. Annoyed. Closed off and wanting nothing to do with me this week. Gwen had been worse than usual after the excursion to the hospital. James had no idea what happened, but he figured Sarah Welsh had something to do with it.

But that wasn't why he had asked to see Cassandra.

"She's doing well. I believe she's at the gym right now." Gwen lived at the gym three days a week. She claimed it was the best way to do something productive and healthy while hanging out with friends and having a social life. Most of her friendships in higher society had originated at the exclusive downtown gym. *I can't complain. She stays super fit, and I reap those benefits.* "But, you know, she's had a rougher year than most."

Cassandra's lips pursed. Did she know what James meant without needing him to explain it? "I'm sorry to hear that."

"Are you?"

The sense of betrayal was instantaneous on Cassandra's face. The waitress saved her any extra embarrassment by showing up with that cosmopolitan.

"Of course I'm saddened to hear that your partner is having such a hard time." Cassandra lowered her voice. Rarely did she sound so… rigid. *Not sure I'm a fan. Then again, I probably brought this out of her.* "I never meant for Gwen to go through so much. I didn't think…"

Yes, yes, she hadn't thought. Somehow, that didn't surprise James. Everything, from going behind James's back to have his child, to magically deciding to include him in his son's life, was devoid of any real thought process. James had made more thoughtful decisions when he was drunk off his ass in college. As far as he knew, though, none of his piss-poor decisions ruined anyone's life.

There was a thought. *Had* Gwen's life been ruined?

Only then did James realize that silence had come to their intimate table. This wasn't what he had wanted. When he texted Cassandra half an hour ago, it was to clear the air and maybe get back on track as tentative friends instead of estranged co-parents.

"I'm sorry." James didn't know what he was apologizing for. Certainly not for thinking of Gwen during a meeting like this. "We've gotten off on the wrong foot here."

"Have we? All I did was ask about Gwen. Your partner. I would assume that was a safe if not polite thing to ask about."

How many people did Cassandra act this way around? James would have found it delightful a few years ago. *This* was the woman he remembered from his adolescence. Cassandra's sense of humor was usually much more restrained than James's, but she wasn't opposed to leaving a caustic remark here and there. James liked to think it was her uptight upbringing that made her more prone to calculated zingers instead of the slapstick jokes he loved the most.

"I suppose Gwen is a bit of a soft spot right now."

"I'm sorry to heart that." Cassandra cut him off before he could open his mouth again. "But if you asked me here solely to make me uncomfortable, I'm afraid you've wasted your time. I've run out of the ability to feel any level of discomfort."

James cleared his throat. "I promise, that wasn't my intention."

Sighing, Cassandra said, "I don't know how many times I can apologize, James. What's done is done. Do I regret the birth of my child? Never. I could never regret the act of bringing him into this world. What I do regret, however, is how it came about. I'm not ashamed to have used the methods I did, but how it involved you? I'm sorry. I'll always be sorry about that."

"You knew what you were doing."

"I did, to an extent." Cassandra shrugged. The barrette in her hair slid further down one of her long, curly locks. "My mother made the suggestion. I talked to your father about it. They assured me that you were on board."

The corners of James's mouth twitched. "You never once thought to ask *me* about it? You made me a father without my consent. It would've been one thing if we ever…" He couldn't bring himself to say it. Mostly, he didn't want to spur on any fantasies Cassandra may have still harbored. "There's always a risk when you're intimate with someone. But *we* had no risk, Cassie. We were never more than friends."

Her crestfallen countenance was the type of look that had seduced half the men in the city. *But not me. I was always in the other half.* "I know that, thank you. I didn't… deep down, I think I knew that you had no knowledge of what our families arranged. Besides, you had your life with Gwen, and I didn't want to disturb that. I had the worst kind of tunnel vision."

"Babies?"

"You don't understand, James. My life is… was… a wreck. I was in a really dark place for several years. We grew apart because of it."

For most of his twenties, James assumed he grew apart from his childhood friend because they had become adults with their own lives and paths. They had gotten along as children, but did that mean they would get along as adults? Everyone expected them to get married. There were jokes about it when they were barely older than ten and playing pranks on maids. James hadn't thought about it much back then. He wasn't the kind of little boy that found girls gross or the thought of growing up to get married a terrifying thought. He often accredited his young friendship with Cassandra as helping him navigate those gendered waters. But he never once thought about marrying her. Let alone kissing her or *experimenting* with her. She was his friend. Like his sister. An untouchable bond that would only be perverted if they ever ended up in bed together.

Other childhood friends discovered different things. Not James. He only ever wanted Cassandra as his friend, even if he recognized how beautiful she was, inside and out. She was the woman he wanted in his wedding party, not in the wedding dress.

He never thought that they might have grown apart because of something going on with her mentally. *It was a natural separation, wasn't it?*

"During that time… I searched for meaning. I've always been the family type, like you." James didn't correct her, because he wasn't sure what he was correcting. "I thought that if I shopped around with boyfriends and fly-by-night lovers, I would fall into a family, you know? I was reckless. Both with my heart and my body."

James needed that whisky now. *How could we be so the same yet so different?* James had been fast and loose with his heart and body in his early twenties, in the randy years before he met Gwen. But he had never seen it as self-destruction. He wanted to sleep with women, so he slept with the ones he found attractive and who would have him. College had been the *worst.* But that was the air in his fraternity. Even his best friend Ian had probably slept with half the women in his repertoire while at college. Once women heard that the handsome boys in Beta Kappa Phi were the sons of billionaires, they lined up to attend the frat parties and get into bed as soon as some nice young man noticed them.

"You mean you would fall into the family way," James said.

"Yes." Cassandra shuddered. "I was lucky my body survived that time. I'm not sure my mental health has, though. I go to a therapist twice a week and have been on a carousel of medications to give myself clarity. I don't know if I've told you, but I had post-partum depression after Patrick was born."

"I'm sorry to hear that."

"It's much better now. The medication has helped immensely." Cassandra's face lit up. "Apparently, it's very common. My mother says she had it with me as well."

"That so?" Another thing that didn't surprise James.

"I firmly believe that my life has changed for the better since having Patrick. But before that…" Cassandra lost the luster in her complexion. "I kept up my old ways even after discovering I was pregnant. It was like a fever dream. Even though I took myself to the doctor and had all these conversations about my health and future with your *father*…"

James sucked in a deep, angry breath.

"…It wasn't real until I started showing. Next thing I knew, my mother took me into hiding, because she didn't want a shitstorm starting because it got out that I was pregnant. She knew how promiscuous I had been. She didn't want any sniff of a rumor coming near us."

"She was afraid I would find out."

"You, and others. Sometimes I'm not sure my mother knows you're an actual person."

"Of course she doesn't. As soon as it was clear I had no intention of dating or marrying you, I ceased to exist as anything more than a sperm donor. Literally."

"James!"

"It's true, isn't it?"

Cassandra looked as if she couldn't believe what he said. Yet how could she deny it? James caught onto those games long before Cassandra ever had the chance, and that's probably what their parents counted on. It was a perfect storm, wasn't it? Cassandra, depressed and vulnerable… and James, too involved in his own life to care what his father did with the old childhood friends. They had both been screwed over. The only difference between them was that Cassandra didn't have a partner to worry about hurting.

"I worry about our son." Cassandra's chin was propped on her hand. Her drink remained untouched, and her barrette had made it halfway down her hair. "Growing up in a place like that. I don't want to move, especially since he's so young right now, but what can I do if…"

James didn't meter the words forming in the back of his head. "That's why it's important I become a part of my son's life. I'm not only talking about visiting once or twice a week, Cassie. I mean making him a part of *my* life. He's going to need his dad to keep the crazies away."

He had no idea how she would take that. Depending on the day and how she felt getting out of bed, Cassandra would either find that a beautiful sentiment or a pox upon her house. Luckily for James, she sighed in relief and said, "I was hoping you would say something like that. I would have completely understood if you wanted nothing to do with him…"

"How could you say something like that? He's still my son." Every time James visited the boy, Patrick looked more and more like his father. That hair. Those eyes. The little cheekbones. Even the cocky, devil-may-care way Patrick rolled onto his side when confronting a problem was unmistakably *Merange,* like the family name his mother had given him. The biological impulse to protect his own bundle of genetics was strong within James's heart. He could have crossed paths with Patrick on the street and known he was *a son.* Not that it would have done either Patrick or James any good to discover each other that late in life. "If he's going to bear my name," James continued, "he better have some of my influence."

"You know I won't bar you from sharing custody if that's what you want. Right now, I'm the only one with the legal right to say what happens to him. My own mother doesn't have that much power."

"We can cross that bridge if it becomes pertinent, or when he gets older."

"I want you to know that I won't keep you from being a father to our son."

James finished his drink and checked the time. *The gathering starts in an hour. Do I still want to go?* After this, he would need the guy talk. "I'm sure Gwen will come around by then."

Cassandra shared a pensive look. "I hope so, too. The more outside influence, the better."

"You mean that?"

"Of course I mean that. I want nothing but happiness for you and Gwen."

Do you really mean that? Cassandra always had a mote of jealousy in her eye when she spoke of or heard Gwen's name. James supposed that was to be expected, since Gwen was the woman he fell in love with and not Cassandra. That would either mean a tenuous respect between both women, or chaos. *Look at my own parents. They say everything I need to know.*

"Perhaps this is a blessing in disguise." James had been thinking it for a while, but didn't dare bring it up with anyone but Cassandra. "A part of me has always wanted to be a father, but I know that Gwen isn't on the same train as me. I had made peace with it if it meant being with her, but…"

Cassandra was rapt with attention.

"Things happen." That's all James would say on that matter for now.

He tried not to think about it, though. He worried that Cassandra may read the expressions on his face or see the scars on his heart. *Being with Gwen meant giving up fatherhood, unless we took alternative measures.* That meant Gwen had to be on board with it. Something she always flip-flopped on, stating that it didn't matter if she couldn't have kids.

Now James was a father. Gwen never had to worry about the pressure to give him children, whether she wanted them or not. How James's son came to be wasn't ideal, but like Cassandra said, he was here now. Time to man up and be a father, even if James wasn't prepared.

But Gwen hasn't taken to being a stepmother very well…

"Maybe this won't be so bad." That's what James kept telling himself. Now he merely vocalized it to the mother of his only child, a woman he never thought about marrying in a million years, let alone dating on an intimate enough level to create a child. "Maybe there is a God, and He's facilitating our fates because He's got nothing better to do. Everything happens for a reason, right?"

James got up. Cassandra remained seated. The strange look she gave him suggested that she had no idea what the hell he was talking about.

"Your barrette is…" James hesitated before outstretching his hand and unclipping the barrette from Cassandra's hair. She sat back in slight surprise as the rose dropped into her palm. James's hand was slow in its return to his side. "Sorry. Watched it fall out of your hair ever since you sat down."

Cassandra closed her hand over the barrette. "Thank you. Would've hated to lose it."

"Well, I…" Something choke him. The truth. A bitter, strange truth he had yet to share with anyone outside of his relationship. His parents didn't know. His best friend didn't know. Hell, James only thought about it once or twice a year when it became legally pertinent to discuss with the accountant and his own partner. "Actually, there's something you should know."

Maybe telling Cassandra was the right step toward getting help with his relationship. James could take Gwen to a couple's counselor five times a week and get nowhere. Or he could go to the woman he trusted with the upbringing of his son. All he needed was the reassurance that she wouldn't tell a soul.

"Pinky swear, Cassie." He held out his left pinky. "Like when we were kids. You can't tell anyone what I'm about to tell you."

She lifted her hand and hooked her finger around his. "Pinky promise." A little grin crossed her face. "If I never told anyone about the time you urinated yourself when we were nine, I won't tell anyone this."

I had completely forgotten about that. Thanks, Cass. "It has to do with Gwen." James sat back down. He would be late to his fraternity meetup, but this was more important. He could talk to his old frat brothers anytime. An opportunity to open himself up to someone only came once or twice a year. "It's why I will do anything to stay with her and make her happy."

Cassandra rubbed her finger against her lips, eyes narrowing in anticipation. "Go on."

James ordered another drink and a snack to go with it before daring to dive into that deep and dark rabbit hole.

CHAPTER 9

GWEN

"Heard you had lunch with Cassandra recently."

Gwen continued to pick at her dinner while James dropped his napkin. He bent down to pick it up and toss it into the dirty linen basket in the center of the dining table. *I bet his mother is appalled we have a dirty napkin basket right on our dinner table.* When it was only the two of them eating at that table, what did it matter? Gwen's family would throw those things right in the trash behind the table!

"First of all," James said with a soft, even tone, "it wasn't lunch. We had drinks at one of the lounges. Privately." He spared his partner a stern look. "Where did you hear that? I had hoped nobody spied on us for the whole ten minutes we talked."

"Oh, calm down." Gwen picked up her wineglass, expertly paired with the roasted rosemary chicken and potatoes on her plate. "I know you're not wooing her."

"Wooing? God, you're turning into my mother."

James sniped a piece of chicken off his fork before letting it clatter to his plate. A fresh napkin touched his lips. Gwen caught herself staring at the flick of his tongue against his stubble. A tiny piece of rosemary lingered at the corner of his mouth. She took another drink.

"I heard it from Charlotte, who heard it from her mother, who heard it from Francesca Blake, who was at the lounge with her old-crone girlfriends talking about who Hyacinth Winchester will pick to inherit her vast fortunes when she eventually chokes."

"It's going to be Michael Winchester," James said with certainty. "Boy's been groomed since he was old enough to toddle." He grabbed his wineglass and washed down his potatoes. His lackadaisical way of leaning back in his hand carved chair wearing a tight green T-shirt and freshly pressed gray sweatpants was going to destroy Gwen. She had been ovulating for the past two days, and every time she looked at her partner, she swore she was about to explode.

Too bad they had both been in a mood. When the chance came to have sex, one or both of them were either too tired or too put out to do anything about it.

"So, what were you and Cassandra talking about?"

"Our son, of course."

Gwen continued to stare at her plate, glass of wine in her hand. *Our* son, he had said. Once the shock of fatherhood had died down, James was quick to embrace his new role as a father. Sometimes, Gwen worried, he was too quick. *I knew he wanted kids, and yet I got mixed up in a relationship with him.* Was it because Gwen never thought it would last this long?

It's not that I hate the idea of having kids… Preferably kids that had already been born, though. Gwen had a lifelong fear of pregnancy and childbirth due to watching her aunt almost die with every child she had. Didn't help that one of the more traumatic childbirths happened in Gwen's living room when she was old enough to "help out" during the emergency. *Sometimes I still see all that blood and the* guts *and it's a miracle I don't wretch.* Of course, it hadn't been real guts. But child-Gwen had no idea what else it could have been. Far as she was concerned, her aunt had been cut open and left to rot in a kiddie pool.

Aunt Rachel was still alive today, and had another kid after that, but some images could not be erased from impressionable minds.

"I take it Patrick's on the mend," Gwen said, desperate to stop thinking of afterbirth and raw umbilical cords. *Gag. Why am I eating chicken?* It was kinda the same color…

"He's doing well. I'm supposed to go see him tomorrow." James tapped his fingers against his glass before looking up at his partner. "Do you want to go with me?"

She didn't hesitate. "I don't think that's a good idea."

James drummed his knuckles on the table before getting up without another word.

Gwen tossed her napkin down with a sigh. When the chef popped out from the kitchen to see how dinner went over, she thanked him for another wonderful meal and asked that James's leftovers be saved for breakfast.

She wasn't in a hurry to chase James down. He was either in the den or in his office. Based on his mood, Gwen guessed he went to play video games and take his mind off real life. *Me. Take his mind off me.*

She should have gone in there and talked things out. She should have laid out her worries, her concerns, her love for him and what it would mean to change half of what they had ever known. She should have done a lot of things. Then again, so should have James.

Gwen wanted to talk. There were a million issues on her mind. Most of all, what the concept of "family" meant to them going forward.

But she had put up this front for so long that it seemed impossible to simply approach her partner and be heard. James would listen, of course. He'd make sure every word was processed in his brain, and every emotion his partner felt kept close to his heart. Then he would rebuttal with his own concerns and how they included Gwen. That was almost as hard to bear as the worries in Gwen's own heart.

There's a wall between us. Something needs to tear it down.

Two hours later, Gwen pulled herself away from the television and decided it was time to get ready for bed. Odds were good that James was already in bed or sharing the same thoughts. Indeed, Gwen stepped into the master chambers to the sound of running water in the bathroom. Steam filtered through the door, left ajar.

At least he was busy. Gwen could grab her toothbrush without saying a word.

She did not expect to walk into the bathroom to the sight of her partner indulging in certain activities in the shower.

All right, so she should have expected it. Chances weren't that bad, especially if they hadn't had sex that day. (James clearly did not think he was getting any.) Gwen also had sex on the brain.

Raw, passionate, dirty sex. The kind they used to have before lovemaking became a parliamentary procedure.

"Wow." She stood next to the shower door, where steam billowed out, and her partner made eye contact with her, his cock still in his fist. "Going for it, huh?"

The animalistic look in his eyes devoured her whole. Top to bottom, head to toe. In one heated gaze, James reminded Gwen that he was as much of a sexual being as she was.

"Why?" His husky voice was almost drowned out by the sounds of the shower. Water sprayed his chest. His black hair was slick against his scalp, bringing attention to his forehead and the tips of his ears, both usually concealed by his hair. None of this was helped by the shower water dripping down is stomach and to the erection in his hand. "You want to join?"

"Depends. What are you thinking about?"

"You really wanna know?"

No. "Yes."

That was the same boyish grin he had the first time they met – the first time they had sex in the corner of some cramped, outdated office in the back of a bar. Gwen fell for it every single time, hard cock in front of her or no. "You."

"Liar."

His mouth curved into a salacious *O*. "What makes you think I don't fantasize about you when I'm masturbating?"

"Because I'm not stupid. I'm also not here to police your thoughts." Gwen reached her arm up the shower door. She was wearing a white T-shirt and nothing underneath. *Countdown to when my tits stick out, 3… 2…* "You wanna jack it thinking about the actress we saw in a movie yesterday, be my guest."

"I only fantasize about you."

"Oh, stop."

"You want me to paint you a picture?" James turned around and leaned against the shower wall. His hand slowly moved up and down his shaft, enough to keep him hard, but nothing was going anywhere. *Lord, is he waiting for me?* Gwen glanced down. Oh, look. Nipples. "I was thinking about that time we rented a playroom in New York City. You wore that cute little black bunny mask."

"And stockings. And boots the length of my legs."

"Oooh, yes, you did."

Gwen couldn't help but smile. "You ripped my brand-new stockings."

"They were in the way."

"*You* were in the way of me enjoying how good I looked in those stockings. I've never found a pair half as flattering on these legs." All her days in the gym meant she had some fairly meaty calves. They were hell to dress up in nice socks and tights. If the clothes didn't oddly accentuate her hard-earned muscles, they burst open at the first sign of friction. James liked taking that to his advantage.

Why was that the kind of memory that warmed Gwen's heart?

"Stick with me, kid," James said, still holding his cock as if it were in danger of getting away from him, "and I'll find you a new pair."

"You've been saying that for years."

He prowled through the shower steam, like a strong, cunning jaguar paying no mind to the jungle in its wake. *Both are just as hot, right?* Gwen leaned against the shower door when her partner arrived. He finally released his cock and tipped her chin up with wet fingers.

"I'll say whatever you want me to say, if it means getting you in this shower with me."

"Bet you'd like that." Gwen cleared her throat before she gave her budding arousal away. Not fair for James to still be so hot after all these years. *Not fair* for him to know how to get to her like this. Cock of the head. A little smirk. His manhood on full display, ready for *her* to pounce upon as soon as she lost control of her actions. "You just want to call me a dirty girl."

"Oh, Gwenny," he said with a purr. "You're far from dirty. You're positively sparkling."

"All right, that's the hard-on talking."

"No, if he were talking, it would sound like *you hot, you pretty, you be naked now?*"

"Yes, that does sound more like him."

James was only a small reach away. His hand crawled up the shower door, putting everything, from the breadth of his naked chest to the Adonis belt of his pelvis on display. Gwen didn't bother looking away. Why, when this was the greatest thing she had seen in days?

"Well?" James asked. "You coming in here or not?"

"If I don't come in, what will you do?"

"Go right back to what I was doing before you interrupted."

"*Interrupted?* You sure that's the word you want to use?"

"Oh, absolutely. I was edgin', Gwen. Had this great image of you in those stockings and that sheer bunny mask with your ass up in the air and your pretty pink pussy begging for it."

Gwen's eyebrows may have gone up in amusement, but heat settled in her groin. *Damn him for putting into words what I was already thinking.* They had never been shy about sharing their sexual fantasies or being open with their predominant kinks. That was one of the biggest reasons Gwen readily got into a relationship with James after they started dating. He was easy to talk to. They didn't always have much in common, but the communication lines were open, and James was one of the greatest listeners Gwen had ever met.

The fact he was so hot that she drooled every time he walked by in one of his tailored suits or – worse – sauntered in baggy sweatpants and not much else helped. Until a year ago, their sex life had been as vibrant as ever. Loving each other was akin to making that love over and over.

She wanted to make love now. She just didn't know what kind of message that would send – to him, or to her own subconscious.

"What would happen if I joined you in this steamy shower?"

James bit his lip in anticipation. "I've got a lot of shit I want to tell you to do."

"Oh! So it's like that?" How typical. James would take his first opportunity to dominate her. He might as well have given her an ultimatum: let him tell her what to do, or walk away.

Wait… was it an ultimatum? If Gwen told him to try again some other day… would there be another day?

He was open. Raw. Inviting her back into his world with no questions asked. All she had to do was wrap her arms around him and feel that wave of erotic love all over again.

Remember how exhilarating it was the first time you two fooled around? Did she mean at the bar, or back at his place on their first real date? James had taken her to the planetarium and shared his reverent awe for astronomy. Photos of planets, interactive constellation creators, and even the cosmos-themed café, where they ate buttery popcorn and went over Gwen's history as a bartender, had been full of laughs and the incredulous disbelief that they might be a normal couple one day.

We had sex all night long. Once James got wind that Gwen liked it a little rough, he went for it. Even threw in some brusque commands and suggested she one day give him her total submission. It had been tempting, of course. This was a man with a million dollars at his disposal and the wherewithal to know when he was too foolish to bear. But Gwen wasn't the type to simply hand her boyfriend the keys to her most well-kept secrets, the ones she stored in the depths of her heart. She had said, "*I'll give you mine if you give me yours.*" Most men would have balked. James? He had said, "*I've been waiting all my life for a woman to say that.*"

Gwen didn't wield the whip as often as her partner did, but she didn't want to. She simply wanted the security in knowing that she *could.* While most of their friends knew that they switched in the bedroom, none of them knew to what extent feisty Gwen could take her infatuated lover. Yeah, it had been months – maybe two years – since they went that far.

She placed her hand on his warm cheek and said, "I've got a lot of shit I wanna tell you to do, too."

James grinned. "Wait your turn, honey."

"You get to go first?" Her fingers slowly descended his chest, following the happy trail and ending up dangerously close to his erection. Not once did James flinch. He was that in control of his physical responses, although God only knew what went on in his head. *More visions of me in torn stockings, begging him to fuck me.* To be fair, that had actually happened. Although James forgot the handcuffs keeping her fists close to her heart. "That's not fair."

"It's fair if I say it is."

The bite in his voice was either desire or frustration. Didn't those often go together, though? "You think you get to stand here in the shower and jack off without me around? *That's* not fair."

"Didn't think you cared to visit."

Gwen pushed him back into the shower. The hot water spray hit her, instantly turning her skin pink and flattening her white T-shirt against her breasts. She was lucky she was barefoot when she stepped into the shower.

"I *always* care to visit."

The shower door shut behind her. Gwen didn't give a shit that she still wore her shirt and shorts. All the better for her partner to see what she had beneath them while the water continued to dampen her hair and drip down her muscular calves.

James kissed her. Gwen threw herself into the moment, scrambling for a hold on his shoulders and insisting that he not redirect the hard cock digging into her abdomen. There was plenty of time to move. They could start by hitting the back wall and feeling each other up.

"Damn," James growled, hands clutching her ass through her soaking wet cotton shorts. *Not the only thing wet by now.* "I forgot how needy you could get after it's been a while."

"Shut up and fuck me."

"Nuh-uh." James held her arms close to her torso. The raw power surging through his muscles made Gwen melt beneath the heat of the showerhead. "My turn first, remember? If you want it, you have to work for it."

Bastard. Gwen hated it – as in, she loved it – when he turned into a bossy bastard full of bravado and machismo. It was perfect in the right situations. Like this one. *Go ahead and make me remember what makes this worth it.*

She fell in love with him all over again in that instance. The ardor in his eyes, the desire in his grip… they were both for her. Only her.

"What do you want, then?" It took no effort to soften her voice. She wanted him to hear that side of her, to witness the moment her eyes fluttered shut and she became his all over again.

James glanced down and then back into her eyes. "Been a while since you laid it on me."

"Laid what?" Gwen ran her hands down his sides, delighting in the way his skin reacted to her touch. Perhaps it was the hot water making him shudder like that, but she desired to think it was *her.* "My love? My adoration? My *mouth?*"

"Yeah. All of those."

Their grins instantly matched each other's in strength. Good to know that they were on the same wavelength after so long.

"That's right." James could go from mischievous master to domineering alpha-lord in half a second. That was the kind of self-control that made women like Gwen really, *really* get down on their knees. The shower floor was not the kindest soul to assist Gwen's comfort, but she was also no stranger to digging her knees near her partner's feet and leaving a trail of tender kisses all over his pelvis. "Get your hair all wet for me."

She couldn't tell if that was a jest. With James, it almost always was. "You want me wet from top to bottom, is that it?"

"I have got the most fantastic view from up here. Seriously, from now on, I command you to shower with a white T-shirt on."

Gwen grabbed the base of his cock, a hiss escaping his teeth. Lesser men would've finished right there, especially if they had been "busy" before Gwen got there. Not James. She knew how well he held himself back, how far he could push himself before pain overtook pleasure – Gwen had personally seen him to that edge and back many, many times.

In those years, Gwen had fellated his cock countless times. She was so familiar with his maximum size that she knew best how to run her tongue down the length of his shaft and relax her jaw to accommodate the girth coming into her mouth.

There had been a learning curve, long, long ago. Gwen was experienced at oral pleasures, but James was one of the biggest men she ever serviced. Even a woman like her had to sometimes take it easy and let her tongue do most of the work.

Growls loud enough to drown out the spray of shower water encouraged her to swallow as much of him as she could. By the time Gwen was overwhelmed by musk and the heat of his skin, she had forgotten everything that had bothered her over the past year.

What year? Hadn't they always been this close, this reverent of each other's bodies and the urges they cultivated? Gwen couldn't remember a time when they didn't embrace each other's pleasure and make the most out of lovemaking. From the day he slammed her against the office wall and pounded her until he came, Gwen had been his.

The most blessed thing about it was that their possession of one another wasn't vocalized until well into their relationship. It didn't need to be. They simply felt it, and it was.

She worshipped this man. He idolized her. Together, they were in an endless loop of need and devotion, the perfect balance few couples ever achieved.

Gwen might as well worship the fuck out of him right now.

That was part of the game, after all, and they were always playing little games both in and out of the bedroom. As much as Gwen loved the dominant way James threw himself around his own house, she loved it even more when she could crack that façade and get a silly grin of disbelief out of him. Which he bestowed upon her when she sucked him so hard that he almost lost it right then and there.

She lived for those moments. The look into his softened heart. Many people knew how amicable James Merange could be, but they often didn't see this side of him. Good. Because Gwen wanted it all for herself.

Wasn't that what this past year had been about? Wanting to keep James for *herself?*

He was close to climax, and would soon reach a point that even he couldn't prevent. James sensed it as well. He commanded her to stop, and she did so without hesitation, the shower water rinsing away anything lingering between her mouth and his cock.

James shut off the shower. Gwen reached for the hem of her shirt to rip it off, but when he asked her to keep it on, she didn't question it. While she was still on her knees, waiting for him to tell her what to do next, James grabbed a towel and dried himself off, careful to not touch his erection. Gwen looked on in desperate need for her own relief. After all, she could no longer blame the shower for how hot she was.

The towel landed on the bathroom floor. James pulled Gwen up by the hands and took her into his arms, carrying her to their bed in the other room and dropping her, wet clothes and all, on top of the comforter.

The thrilling ride in his arms only made her more desperate.

Without a word, James ripped off the cotton shorts still clinging to her thighs. Her exposed pussy and the cold air hitting her heat made her sigh into the bedspread; him prying her legs apart and bringing her naked flesh to his all but guaranteed that this was about unfettered possession.

Gwen let out a cry of submission when he entered her.

The white T-shirt made sure the bed was damp beneath her. James's hands smacking her ass and grabbing her breasts through the thin strip of cloth keeping them tucked against her chest made her relent to his whim and agree that she was his, now and forever.

He grabbed her slick hair. She spread her legs and enticed him to go deeper. Together, they were one.

James held out long enough for Gwen to scream into the bedspread, her body rolling in climax now that she had what she subconsciously wanted for so long. She sucked him in and ensured that he wouldn't leave her when orgasm finally got him.

He didn't pull out. If anything, he made sure *she* wouldn't go anywhere when he pinned her down by the shoulders and grabbed her hip, immobilizing her thrashing body.

The heat came quick. Every burst of his cock and groan in his throat was an announcement to the world that she could never, ever belong to anyone else.

Five minutes later, when her mind was her own again, she made good on his promise to take turns. James wasn't going anywhere until he knew that he would also never belong to any other woman.

CHAPTER 10

JAMES

"Wildest night in a whole year." James threw himself across the couch by the large bay window overlooking the busy avenue crowded with cars and lined with pedestrians. But that was several stories below. Up there, in Ian's high-rise condo that had more square feet than most starter homes, the noise pollution was non-existent, and the sunlight streamed without obstruction from the building across the street. James had dropped by to let his friend borrow something, but stayed for a drink and to shoot the heavenly breeze. Because when Ian commented that James seemed to be in a fantastic mood, it was only natural for James to *agree.*

Ian sat in a chair on the other side of the coffee table. He had tossed aside his jacket before sitting, something James should have replicated before wrinkling his against his friend's couch. *Don't care. That's what dry cleaning is for.* James, like Ian, had finished most of his business by lunch that day. Ian was settling in for an afternoon at home and a dinner with his girlfriend. James combatted the crazier corners of his imagination that regaled him with promises of tropical getaways and diamond earrings for the woman he loved most. Such were their natures. James could always count on Ian to indulge him. Likewise, Ian would act as the voice of reason when James inevitably plowed full steam ahead into his ideas.

"Seriously. Wildest night." James cupped his hands behind his head and gazed at the sunlit ceiling. Ian's cat, which had a Gaelic name James could never hope to pronounce, hopped onto the back of the couch and dangled its fuzzy tail above James's head. "I'd tell you some of the shit we did to each other, but it'd push your TMI boundaries." He said that with a giant grin.

"Highly doubt she did anything to you that Kathryn's never done to me," Ian muttered. He was, after all, the man dating a professional Domme. James and Gwen may have switched when the moment suited, but Gwen would never call herself a Domme.

"Don't be sure about that." James reveled in the memories from two nights ago. Two blissful nights of making love to his partner, catching up after a year's worth of frustration and angst. *We really hit a breakthrough. I'm not sure why, and I'm not sure how, but I'll be damned if we go back to where we were before.* James hadn't been this happy since he realized he was in love with Gwen. How long ago had that been? How much had he come to rely on Gwen's love to feel complete?

"Then, you're right. I'm good with losing out on a few details." Ian clicked his tongue and summoned his cat to his side. First, though, the frisky feline had to hop off the couch. Instead of leaping over James or going around him, the little kitty bounded off his diaphragm and plopped onto the carpet. "You didn't have any problems walking in here, but you're a stronger man than I when it comes to certain things."

"I'm lucky that my prostate doesn't hide." Nope. It sure didn't. James's grin grew even larger to think about it.

"Yup. TMI, man."

"You know what I should do?" James said, changing subjects. "I need to throw a party for Gwenny. Her birthday isn't too far away. I could *totally* throw her the birthday bash of the century. Still time left to rent the best venue on the block. I'll invite everyone she's ever had a pleasant conversation with. And her parents, I suppose."

"Leaves your parents out."

James didn't need reminding of his father's existence. "No. My father is definitely not invited. Maybe my mother. She likes Gwen."

Ian considered that statement before saying, "But your mother isn't the one pulling the strings behind the scenes, right? Not like my mother would."

No, not every boy had a mother like Ian's, who made it her personal mission in life to drink every drop of gossip and get in her son's face about every little thing, from who he dated to what business move he was thinking of making next. It was no secret that Ian's mother adored Kathryn and urged her to marry Ian as soon as possible. Of course, Kathryn was an heiress – possibly the wealthiest and most highly regarded heiress in the whole city. What well-to-do mother *wouldn't* want her son marrying someone like Kathryn? If the Meranges could have swung it, no doubt they would shove James in Kathryn's direction.

"You're right. My mom has almost noooo say in anything." James failed to see what difference that made to his happiness in the moment. "Not the point. What I need right now is help party planning."

Ian picked up his cat the moment a key hit the lock to his front door. He turned his head in mild interest before looking back in

James's direction. *Perfect timing, Kathryn.* She entered her boyfriend's condo using her copy of his key. A bag from the healthy grocer's down the street hung from one arm while she balanced a bottle of wine in another. *Never mind. My father would hate her. She doesn't command servants to carry her groceries for her.*

"Hey." Kathryn closed and locked the door behind her. The cat perked up on Ian's chest and stared at her until she agreed to come over and stroke its back. Her eyes never left James lying prostrate on the couch. "Sorry. Didn't know you had company, babe."

Ian shrugged, as if to say, "*It's James. Does he count as company? Huh.*"

"Apparently," Ian began, pinning his cat back down to his abdomen, "James and Gwen are on the mend."

"According to *you?*" she asked James. Her nude-colored heels carried her to the counter by the kitchen. The shopping bag hit the black marble countertops, and her purse landed on the nearest stool. When Ian said he was having dinner with Kathryn that night, James was not expecting them to *cook*. But, also according to Ian, Kathryn had been on a healthy cooking and eating kick for the past… year? Two years? Since realizing she had someone she wanted to grow old with?

Damn. That was beautiful. Good thing James had one of those people, too.

"We've had, uh, a good week so far."

Kathryn rolled her eyes but couldn't suppress her snort of laughter when she caught that cheeky grin on James's face. "She finally pegged you again, huh?"

James laughed. Ian turned his head so quickly that he almost snapped his neck off his body – the cat certainly did not appreciate the jostling experience it now suffered. "We don't take kindly to that kind of talk 'round here," Ian said, utilizing the kind of speech they often heard on TV, yet using his everyday upper-class accent. "Not when it gives you ideas."

"Pshaw." Kathryn began putting groceries away in the fridge and cupboards.

"Things are definitely looking up in Casa de Merange," James said. "Which reminds me. I'm going to throw Gwen a big birthday bash, and you *must* come, Kathryn. I'm telling you this now before I forget you're one of her best friends. Because she can't invite you to a party if she doesn't know it's happening."

"A surprise party? For Gwen?" Kathryn shut the refrigerator with a laugh. "You're telling me about it in the hopes I spill the beans, aren't you?"

"No, that would be detrimental to the *surprise.*" James sat up with a new thought. "Unless you tell her a fake story. Oh! You could tell her that I told *you* I wanted to fly her to Hawaii for her birthday. Then the real surprise could be…"

"A Hawaiian-themed party at the airport," Ian said. "That would go over *really well.* You should do that. Make sure Kathryn's roped into it, yup."

"Honestly," she said, "propose to her. That would put a shock in everyone's system."

She was still laughing, though both James and Ian were silent. The cat yawned, stretched across Ian's chest, and hopped down to fuck off to the library on the other side of the condo. Ian didn't move. James pretended he still had breath in his lungs.

"What?" Kathryn held out her hands, one holding a loaf of freshly made garlic bread, and the other a jar of $10 spaghetti sauce. "I wasn't serious. Sheesh." She placed both the bread and the jar on the island counter. Bags rustled. She tossed her hair over her shoulders. "Don't worry, buddy," she said to James, "Gwen's made it quite clear she would kill you if you ever do a public proposal."

Ian hid his cough of shock with a guffaw. James, meanwhile, simply sat up on the couch and inhaled a deep breath. *Might as well tell her too.* Except Gwen would find out about it, and if there was one thing James and Gwen swore to one another, it was to not tell *anyone* their big secret.

Too bad James had told Cassandra.

"Well…"

James had barely figured out what he wanted to say when his phone rang. The chimes of his ringtone made Ian jerk in his seat and Kathryn roll her eyes at the interruption. James grabbed his phone and hoped it was an honest-to-God emergency.

He quickly rescinded that hope when he saw Cassandra's name on the incoming calls list.

"Sorry." He got up from the couch and followed the cat into the library. Ian and Kathryn gave him space. James didn't bother to shut the door. Not when the cat glared at him from its bed.

He took the call and held his phone up to his head.

"Yes?" *Please don't be about Patrick… please don't be about Patrick.*

It wasn't

"James," Cassandra said with her airy voice. It sent a shiver down his spine. A shiver of dread. "You need to head to your family's home right now. My mother left five minutes ago, muttering that she was going to meet Gwen there."

James furrowed his brows. "Excuse me? Why in the world is your mother going to meet Gwen at *my* family's house?" That didn't make any sense. Hell, Gwen going to meet Sarah Welsh *anywhere* didn't make sense! Why would Gwen do something like that without informing her partner?

"I'm not sure what's going on," Cassandra continued, "but my mother was rather pleased with herself, and we both know that might mean trouble."

James hung up one minute later. He shot out of the library with the words, "I've gotta go," on his lips. Ian followed him to the front door without saying anything.

"*Don't* tell Kathryn." Those were James's parting words before he left. He didn't stick around long enough to hear if Ian clung to his word.

CHAPTER 11

GWEN

She emerged from the back of the cab with bile in her throat and a bad feeling in her stomach. As soon as the door snapped shut behind her, the cab driver pulled away from Merange Manor, as if the staff would come running out to chase them with the fires of fury burning at their heels.

To be fair, that's how Gwen felt when she looked up at the imposing mansion looming beneath gray storm clouds. *I should have worn a thicker sweater.* But when Gwen was summoned to Merange Manor at the last minute, she threw on the first sensible outfit she could find. The Meranges would either be pleased with her blazer and slacks or they could rot.

Hell, they could rot anyway!

Gwen was under strict instruction to not inform James of this meeting until told otherwise. That command had come from Ophelia, who insinuated she wanted to plan a surprise for her son and required Gwen's expert opinion. *I heard Albert in the background, telling her what to say.* Ophelia's tone also hadn't inspired much confidence. One of those days, Gwen would have a long, *long* conversation with Ophelia about her options in her marriage. She often wondered if it were possible to oust Albert from his family home and take it over with James. Ophelia could stay, but the puppet master needed to *go.*

Whatever was going on here, it probably wasn't good. But, okay… Gwen would agree to not tell her partner until she had good reason, if that's what it took to get to the bottom of this.

"Good afternoon, Ms. Mitchell," the butler greeted. He gestured for Gwen to enter the grand foyer, but his body language broadcasted that she was *not* to wander. Or at least she assumed that's what it meant when she saw one of the maids standing before a closed door. "Mr. Merange is awaiting you in the study."

"The study, huh?" Wasn't that the door the young lady guarded? Interesting. Gwen hadn't spent much time in Mr. Merange's study. Why would she? She only came to this house when she had to, and Albert wasn't the type to take his daughters-in-law on a tour of his more private places. (Otherwise, they would have even bigger problems.)

"May I take your jacket?"

"No need. It's quite chilly in here." Gwen tightened the strap of her purse over her chest and showed herself to the study. The butler gritted his teeth to see her act so informally in a house that was not hers. How could the help formulate their own opinions of Gwen when she rarely came around and had such *winning* supporters in the Merange family?

The maid stepped out of the way, hand clasping the doorknob. "Will you require any refreshment, Ms. Mitchell?" Her tone implied that Gwen did *not* need any refreshments. At all.

"No, thank you." Gwen's knuckles whitened against her purse. "Although I have one question for you before you open that door."

The maid cocked her head. "Yes, ma'am?"

"Will I see *only* Mr. Merange in his study? Or does he have another guest here today?"

"Afraid I don't follow, ma'am."

Gwen dropped her friendly façade. None of these people were on *her* side. They never had been from the moment their boss insinuated she was a nuisance to only be tolerated until his only child had his fill of her and moved on to better pastures. For all Gwen knew, he told his staff that she killed kittens in her spare time. Kicked over sand castles. Dumped buckets of spiders in the middle of playgrounds. All while cackling gleefully, of course. "You know exactly what I mean."

The maid sniffed. "Mr. Merange has another guest. That's all I'll say."

The fact she said *guest* instead of correcting Gwen's assumptions that Ophelia was not on the other side of the door told Gwen everything that she needed to know. "Thank you. Let me get this over with, please."

"Go on!" came Albert's voice from the other side of the door. "Let her in!"

Two seconds later, the door opened, and Gwen was far from surprised.

There sat Albert behind his stalwart desk made of priceless woods that were both earthy in their illusions and masculine in their *delusions.* He was every bit the kind of patriarch every new money woman hated to encounter on her ascent to the top of the social food chain. The light hair of his graying scalp reminded Gwen that he had been on Earth decades longer than her feeble mind could comprehend. He knew things. Had *seen* things. Couldn't she see the lines of wisdom etching his face? Who was *she* to tell him that she knew better than he did? She was an outsider. An imposter. She may have been with James for several years by now, but she knew that her time was up, didn't she?

Was that everything she figured out *before* seeing Sarah Welsh sitting in one of the chairs before Albert's desk? Almost.

"Oh, wonderful." Gwen wasn't shocked that the maid shut the door. Locked in a room with Sarah Welsh and Albert Merange? Had Gwen died and gone to hell? "Two of my favorite people."

"Rather disappointed you're already forgoing cordiality, Ms. Mitchell." Albert motioned to the empty chair next to his mistress of however many damned years. "At least do it for our guest."

"I thought I was the guest, Albert." Gwen plopped into the chair. While on her way to her partner's family home, she bolstered herself up to be as polite and well-mannered as possible in front of the man who made her life hell. Once she saw Sarah and their intentions to gang up on her, though? All bets were off. Gwen might as well be herself and air out her frustrations with these two people who barely had *anything* to do with her.

She had a feeling that was about to change, again.

"Besides," she said to the man cringing at the informal use of his first name, "I insist that you call me Gwen. Rather odd that I've been with your son for so long and you still call me Ms. Mitchell, isn't it? Almost like we have all this distance between us."

Albert's teeth ground into oblivion. Sarah hid a scoff of amusement behind her curling knuckles. Together, they looked like the gatekeepers to Gwen's nightmares.

"Gwenyth," Albert said. "How's that?"

"Such a strong, Welsh name," Sarah said with a crack of her knuckles. "You'd fit right in with my family. Not that I suggest it."

Anger bristled down Gwen's spine. *Don't rise to their bait.* That's what they wanted. These two salivated to have Gwen explode in the Merange home. Even better if Albert had to call his security to escort her out. That was exactly what he wanted to report to his son should James swing by and demand to know what he had done to Gwen.

"What can I do for the two of you?" Gwen asked with a smile she only used when working at bars or dealing with someone of the last name Merange – well, someone who didn't have the first name James, anyway. "Surely, it must be important if you called me at the last minute to come meet with you, Albert." She glanced around the room, as if she expected to see someone else there. "Where is Ophelia?"

"She is indisposed."

"Who? Your wife?"

The woman next to Gwen shifted in her seat. *Good. Seethe, you old cow.* Whatever Gwen could do to remind Sarah Welsh she was not Albert's wife? Gwen would do it. But she would have to be careful to not go too far – she didn't want to spoil the fun for herself. "Yes," Albert said through clenched teeth. "My wife is indisposed."

"I do hope she gets better soon. We're supposed to have tea at the country club again next week." Gwen would make sure to invite Ophelia to tea. *I bet she'd love to know about the contents of this conversation.* If it could even be called one.

Albert leaned back in his seat, one leg slung over the other and his demeanor softening as he considered the woman before him. *Go ahead, Albert, try to figure me out.* He'd be sorely disappointed to discover that Ms. Mitchell wasn't easily intimidated.

"Let's get one thing straight, *Gwenyth,*" he said with the spitfire of a man about to rid his family of the cog breaking the entire machine. "You and I are not on friendly terms. We never have been. You know why."

She shrugged. His words stung, but would she let him see that? Would she let them fester in her blood? No. Gwen had better ways to use the last of her energy reserves around these people.

"You don't like me. Of course, I have always been aware of that."

"I've tolerated you. Don't get me wrong, I don't find you absolutely distasteful, Gwenyth, but…"

"I'm not who you imagined for your first and only child."

Albert released the smallest smile he could muster. "You know James. He needs a certain someone to keep him in line."

"Oh, I've always thought I did a good enough job at that." As much as Gwen loved her partner, James could occasionally be a handful. When he had the gumption to prank his friends or parade her in front of them in nothing but a negligee and collar, Gwen plotted how she would get "even" with him. *Don't assume I didn't enjoy his pranks and kinks. But I'll be damned if James doesn't get tastes of his own medicine.*

"Have you? Is that why I hear such scandalous rumors about my son's sex life?"

"As long as it's all consensual, I'm not sure why it matters to you."

"You don't even deny it."

Gwen glanced at Sarah, who remained silent in her seat – yet she always had one keen eye on Gwen, as if she waited for the younger woman to take a misstep and fall flat on her face. "Why would I deny anything that's true? Part of the reason your son and I get along so well after all this time is because we trust one another. And have the same tastes."

"Yes. After all this *time.*"

"Cut to the chase, Albert." Gwen dug her elbows into the arm of her chair and kicked one leg over the other. The tips of her high heels touched the bottom of Albert's desk. "You didn't summon me here in front of your mistress so you could ask me questions about my sex life."

Sarah choked on her own spit. Albert furrowed his brows. He only had angry eyes for Gwen – not a drop of concern for Sarah, who snatched a bottle of water out of her bag and glugged it down until she finally stopped coughing.

"You'd do kindly to not refer to Lady Welsh with such candor." The bastard on the other side of the desk said. "I invited her here to make my offer to you much sweeter."

"An offer?"

"You want to cut to the chase? Fine." Albert placed his palms face-down on his desk. His fingertips brushed against a family portrait taken five years ago. Christmas. It was no accident that the six people in the photo represented the Meranges and their dearest friends, the Welshes. Gwen was nowhere to be seen. *I stood off to the side when they took the picture. The reason James looks so constipated is because he tried to get me in the photo, but everyone refused. Yes, even you, Cassandra.* Gwen had brushed it off because she didn't expect these people to take her seriously even after knowing James for three years and moving in with him. After five years, however, she knew better.

They hated her. Save for James, everyone wanted her gone. Perhaps… even Ophelia. Or, at least, Ophelia wouldn't miss her. That would require a spine and thinking for herself. Maybe expressing a real opinion to her husband here and there. *How did James turn out so relatively well-adjusted?* Their counselor had suggested that James's affinity for the absurd and making people laugh was because he came from a laughless household. But Gwen had heard stories from staff that young Mr. Merange was giggling from the moment he was born. "*I also quickly learned that spanking did not work on that child,*" the former nanny had slyly told Gwen at one birthday party. "*He would go out of his way to get spanked. I think he liked it.*"

Well, yeah, James Merange did like the occasional spank to his toned bottom. But that was one of those details Albert probably dreaded to hear.

"We'll cut to the chase, as you have requested," that man finally continued. "I am asking you – no, telling you – to leave this family as soon as you can conveniently make arrangements."

Gwen popped open her purse and pulled out a tin of mints. She took her time selecting the most appetizing before tossing it into her mouth. Wintergreen exploded between her cheeks.

How refreshing!

"What you really want is for me to dump James."

"Don't act like you haven't been thinking about it."

"What in the world makes you say that?"

Albert merely grinned.

Damnit. Ophelia. She must have said something. Or perhaps Sarah had overheard Gwen and Kathryn talking at the restaurant a few weeks ago. The woman had supersonic bitchiness on her side. Why not supersonic hearing?

"James and I may have hit a rough patch since…" Gwen spared a glare for the woman beside her. "But we're on the mend. Why, by this Christmas we'll be our usual selves."

"Even so, I must ask you to please leave."

"Why?"

"Don't play dumb, Ms. Mitchell." Albert wasn't going to play along with Gwen's casual niceties, after all. "You've had your fun with my son. Seven years is more than long enough. It's time for James to grow up and become a family man."

Although these words came from Albert, Gwen couldn't help but continue to glare at the woman beside her. Sarah filed her nails with a bejeweled stick that was tackier than the peacock pin on her blouse. "Let me guess – his destiny is to marry your daughter and raise *their* child together."

Sarah didn't bother to look at her. "Told you she was smarter than you took her for, Albert. Also a right bitch."

"Does that mean he doesn't take you for being as smart as you are, too?" Gwen flashed Sarah her most dazzling smile. *James paid for these veneers.* When they met, Gwen was still self-conscious about the crooked teeth braces had only made worse as a child. James had paid for everything she wanted at the dentist. Gwen had stopped at straightening and some whitening, however. That was back when she still wasn't used to having so much money at her disposal.

Sarah acted as if she didn't know what Gwen implied.

"Since we're both bitches, after all," she said.

"Ms. Mitchell," Albert said with a growl, "you have no place in my family. That's a fact, and I truly hope I can make you see that."

"*Well,*" Gwen said with a sigh so heavy that she almost spat out her mint, "how blunt."

"I haven't lied. Seven years, and you still don't understand the responsibilities foisted upon my son. He's destined to take over *everything*. Do you know what that means for him?"

Gwen couldn't wait to hear this.

"He needs heirs. *I* need heirs before I can die in peace!"

So much easier to direct her anger toward Sarah instead of the idiot in front of her. "Is that why you conspired to knock up your daughter? Long game. I have to give you props for that."

Sarah slammed her nail file into her lap. "Cassandra is willing to do whatever it takes for this family! Can *you* say the same thing, Ms. Barren Womb?"

The half-melted mint lodged itself in Gwen's throat. Nobody got up to help her when she choked. She wondered if they would have let her die, if it weren't for her saliva exacerbating the melting process and freeing up her airways before she turned blue.

"Where did you hear that?" Gwen asked, her words peppered with haggard coughs.

"What?" Sarah reveled in the panic. "That you're incapable of having children? Everyone knows about it, dear. The moment you turn your back on any group of socialites having a chat, they're gossiping about you. Haven't you noticed? Or do you not have friends beyond Kathryn Alison and Charlotte Williams?"

Of course everyone talks shit about everyone else. Welcome to humanity! Gwen knew better than these two adulterous nimrods that people talked. But how in the world did anyone know about her condition? She had only ever told James that her gyno informed her she would probably never have children, due to several reproductive issues since puberty. All of them had treatable symptoms, but she would have to go to extremes to combat her infertility – and there was no guarantee any of them would work.

He hadn't told some blabbermouth, had he? Why in the world would James tell *anyone* that his partner would need surgeries to get by one day, let alone that she was effectively infertile without considerable intervention? *I never really wanted the whole pregnancy, childbirth, young motherhood thing… it didn't bother me enough to treat it.* She was more worried about chronic pain and metabolic issues.

Now she was worried that half the town knew she was an infertile she-demon. Did that make what Cassandra did even *more* scandalous?

"Quite unfortunate," Albert muttered. "Yet let me assure you that I heaved a sigh of relief when I discovered you were unlikely to trap my son with one of your own."

"At least I would've kept my place," Gwen said with a sneer.

"As a starter wife, to be sure."

"Riiiight." Gwen leaned forward, hands gripping the arms of the chair and hair unceremoniously shrouding her reddening face. "You put up with me as long as James was in his twenties and not knocking me up. Now that he's a little *older* though…"

"And a father," Sarah dutifully reminded her.

Gwen shot her the hottest look to blaze a trail from her eyeballs. "Thank you, Sarah!"

Lady Welsh sniffed in admonishment.

"So because James is now in his thirties and a *father*…" Gwen finally sent her wildfire in Albert's direction, "it's time for him to grow up, buckle down, and marry the mother of the child he never helped create. Did I get that right?"

Nobody said anything.

"Don't suppose you've run this brilliant plan passed him first, huh? Because I don't think James will be amused to know you're once more writing the script to his life."

"James doesn't think ahead," Albert brusquely said. "He's never been good at choosing the next path in his life. That's what his parents are for."

"Right. From what boarding school he went to, to what college and area of study he pursued… even your precious frat. In fact," Gwen regaled in this, "the first time he completely turned his back on your life plan for him was when he moved in with me instead of Cassandra. He's been very open about how much you two tried to push them together."

"It's the perfect match!" Sarah insisted. "Our families deserve to be united. It was decided the moment my daughter was born!"

"Why? Because *you two* couldn't get married without pissing off *your* families?" Albert leaped up from his desk. Gwen continued.

"That's what this has always been about, hasn't it? You two didn't have the balls to tell your own parents to piss off with their arranged marriages, so here you are, making your own children's lives hell."

"Ms. Mitchell!" Albert slammed his hand against his desk. Gwen hated that the sound made her jump in her seat. "The one thing you fail to understand during your tenure as my son's girlfriend? There are *expectations* this high up on the food chain!"

"So you admit you think you're top of the food chain?"

He lowered his pointy nose to hers. "Don't test me, Gwenyth." Jesus, would he make up his mind about what he wanted to call her? "You will never understand what it takes to maintain one's social standing. Let alone one's *business.* Merging with the Welshes is what's best for my family. We are not at the whim of our hearts and loins."

Gwen guffawed. They weren't? Then what was *this* ongoing relationship from hell between Albert and Sarah? The whole reason their families were miserable was because they wouldn't fucking elope when they had the chance! *Forty years of hell. It's not my fault – or James's fault – that you two subjected yourself to this.* While dragging down their unwitting spouses. What year was this again?

"You are the only reason my daughter isn't with James," Sarah insisted. "If you leave him, Cassandra will be there to mend his broken heart."

"Wow. I bet." Gwen figured that the moment she followed her gut and left James, Cassandra would swoop in as the concerned and good-hearted woman ready to assuage the pain in his heart. *With her cunt. Yup.* James claimed to have never even kissed Cassandra, let alone slept with her before. "*She's like a sister to me, Gwenny. It would be so… wrong. I can't see her sexually at all.*" That's what he had told Gwen more than once. She believed him, too.

Not once in the years she had seen them interacting, had Gwen ever witnessed anything less than friendly between James and Cassandra. The Meranges and Welshes played themselves. They forced those two kids together so much that they became siblings, not potential lovers.

How ironic. Especially now that Gwen had decided to *not* leave James, after all.

Even so, she was not in the mood to deal with these asinine people. "At least you're honest about what you're doing," she said. "Can't fault you for that."

"We're also prepared to make it worth your while to leave, if that's what it takes."

Gwen raised her eyebrows. "Both of you, huh?"

"We figured we both had some resources to spare if we pooled them together," Sarah said. "Simply name your price, and we'll go from there."

"You want to pay me off."

"Clearly, you're attracted to the money this lifestyle affords you," Sarah continued with a haughty sigh. "I suggested to Albert that we make this as mutually beneficial as possible. We get you out of our hair, and you get half of the equation you seem to love so much."

"The money, yes?" These people were utterly ridiculous. Did being born into so much wealth and privilege stagnate the human brain? These people wouldn't even stand up for themselves as young adults. Did they think they simply paid it forward to their own children? Monsters. Both of them. "What's the other half the equation?"

"The man himself, of course." Sarah shrugged. "James is quite the specimen, even among his peer group. I don't doubt you were physically attracted to him before the money came into play.

Unfortunately, you'll have to give that up, but we're optimistic that we'll find a decent price to soothe that ache."

Gwen shook her head. "You're both mad. Even if you gang up on me, I won't deny how hard I've worked to make a life with James. Besides…" she sucked in a deep breath that could mean the end of her life, "it's not as simple as walking away from him."

"Why's that?"

Before Gwen could open her mouth and spout the truth she and James had kept close to their hearts for the past two years, the maid threw open the door and shouted, "Mr. Merange! It's…"

It was James, tearing through the foyer on the hunt for whatever his father concocted *this* time.

CHAPTER 12

JAMES

"*Dad!*"

James met his father's eyes the moment he burst into the office. He should've known. His father. Sarah Welsh. *Gwen.*

Together, that was a toxic combination. Meeting in a closed room like this, *and* James wasn't invited? Toxicity leveled up to ground-zero termination.

Naturally, all three responded to his sudden presence with a myriad of reactions. Lady Welsh nearly leaped out of her seat in shock, hand smacked over her heart and a gasp echoing in the large home office her lover had called his *hideaway from the Mrs.* for thirty years. Albert? His countenance burned with an unappreciation for his son the world had yet to see.

Gwen… her face flashed between relief that she didn't have to face this alone… and frustration that her partner dared to sweep in with *her* behind him.

Because James had apparently not come by himself.

Although he did not ask Cassandra to join him on this misadventure, she was soon in the doorway with him, a chastising look bestowed upon her own mother. It was the most active James had seen her in years. Gone was the sweet dormouse that grew on *his* nerves when he simply wanted a straight answer about their son. Now, he was in the presence of the vibrant woman he had once called his closest friend.

Cassandra slammed her foot down and barked at her own mother. "This really has to be the biggest slap in the face you could give our family, Mother." Cassandra brushed off the maid attempting to draw her away from the office threshold. "Conspiring with a man you're not even related to so you can break up his son with his girlfriend? That's low, even for you."

Sarah jumped out of her seat. A vintage Louis Vuitton bag fell from her lap and plopped onto the plush carpet. Gwen glanced at it, but did not move to pick it up. *It's a miracle she's not taking the opportunity to step all over it.* James wouldn't blame her. That bag had probably been bought as an "anniversary" present from Albert.

That man opened his mouth, but like James had interrupted Gwen from saying something, Sarah now came to her own defense when she saw such shame in her child's face.

"Everything I have *ever* done has been for you!"

Gasping, Cassandra turned on her heels and stumbled into the foyer of James's childhood home. *It wouldn't be the first time she's tripped and fallen in this room.* Cassandra still had a scar on her knee from that time she scraped it when she and James were children, playing tag and getting into all sorts of rambunctious trouble. *How many injuries have you sustained because your mother forced us together?* James caught Cassandra before she twisted her ankles. Still, he could not stop the pained sound escaping her lips.

She wasn't in pain because of almost falling to the floor. Cassandra cried out because her mother was the *worst.*

"How could you?" Once she had regained her footing, Cassandra shoved James off her and rounded on the woman in the doorway. Sarah did her damnedest to stand her ground, but one of her crow's feet threatened to fly away at the tone of her daughter's words. Even the distinguished Lady Welsh couldn't handle a woman like Cassandra when she finally put her emotions to use.

Outside of seducing men, anyway.

"Don't claim to do things for me!" Cassandra pulled her bangs out of her face, teeth bared and cheeks puffing in righteous indignation. "Not when you're really doing them for yourself!"

Sarah squared her shoulders, yet that lump traveling down her throat did not inspire confidence. "Watch your mouth, you ungrateful…"

"Ungrateful what? *Child?* I stopped being a child *years* ago! I have a child of my own!" Cassandra balled one of her fists. James wondered if he would have to intervene on the least likely physical confrontation to ever hit New England. The thought of Cassandra hitting *anyone* was absurd. Watching her lash out at her own mother would have sent them into an alternate dimension. "The only reason you still see me as a child is because I let you for so long. But don't delude yourself into thinking that any of your plans are truly for my well-being. They're all because of what *you* want."

Cassandra turned to James.

"Do you know what's going on here?" she asked him. "Our parents won't ever stop trying to get us married because of *their* spineless fuckups."

"How dare you!" Sarah stormed toward her daughter. It took James crossing his arms in consternation and Albert leaping around his desk to make Lady Welsh halt her approach.

"I'm not sure what you've heard on the grapevine, Cassandra," Albert said, both feet now in the foyer. "But I can assure you that your mother and I are far from *spineless.*"

Gwen was the last to raise from her seat and join the rest of them in the foyer. James beheld the clarity in his partner's eyes and instantly felt that mixture of excitement and dread that so often came from being in Gwen's presence during heated confrontations. *Why wouldn't I feel this way? Look at her.* Gwen was brains and beauty rolled into one deadly combination. With a snap of her fingers, she could convince James to prostrate himself on the tiled floors of his childhood home. Why not? If any woman was qualified to take his mother's place as lady of this household, it was the only woman who could fell him with one cold look.

"It's true," she said with an even voice. "These two have balls so big that they were offering me whatever sum I wanted to get the hell out of town."

She said that while maintaining eye contact with her partner, who now dropped his jaw and shot his father an exasperated look. "You *what?*" James had heard of a hundred terrifying stories in the world of patriarchs who did not approve of their sons' girlfriends, but the thought of Albert Merange offering Gwen millions of dollars to dump her beloved and get the hell out of town was… preposterous. *My own father? Daring to do something so stupid?* Oh, who was James kidding? His father had always proven to be an ass. *I thought he was a harmless one!*

Albert had never approved of Gwen, and he made that known from the day James first brought her home. But he had kept his disproval to himself. A knowing look here and there. A pertinent question that raised suspicions. Then, only three years ago, he had dropped the purpose of Gwen's existence entirely. James had foolishly assumed that his father had finally accepted that Gwen was *forever*. That he had, oh, perhaps accepted his son's love for a commoner? Like it mattered anymore! Who were they trying to impress? Friends at the country club? Half the men who made up James's peers married commoners. The others scooped up the few heiresses who weren't train wrecks. *Like Cassandra.* James hated to think that, but that was her reputation in the circles he frequented.

"Well," Albert said with a snort of disdain, "you'll be pleased to know that your woman could not be swayed."

"No shit!" James turned away before he spat at his father's feet. Gwen remained on the other side of the foyer, her serene visage the exact thing James needed right now. But why was she so unfazed by the situation? Had she used the last of her give-a-fuck reserves? Was she so over this charade that she would rather let the waves of bullshit wash over her than fight them head-on? "This might shock you, Dad, but Gwen is more than my girlfriend. She's my…" His words faltered, and it had nothing to do with the unchanging countenance on his partner's face. *You're killing me, Dad.* This man wouldn't understand. He had given up the woman he loved to placate his own parents and to "do the right thing." Maybe Albert thought it had been worth it. The increasing fortunes, the social connections Ophelia brought, the peaceful, *harmonious* households it maintained… until the rumors spread that he continued his affair with the newly-married Sarah. An unspoken rumor that nobody dared to mention in the open, but everyone knew. They were the cautionary tale men muttered into bourbons when debating whether to chase after the woman they weren't supposed to love. "She's my everything."

Albert scoffed. Sarah rolled her eyes.

Gwen smiled.

"She's damn right she's not going anywhere." James stuck his foot into the circle the five of them created. A shaking hand also emerged from the cuff of his jacket. Not that he would let it *shake* in front of his father. A man standing up to his own father couldn't show a hint of weakness. It meant he wasn't ready, and James had been *ready* since the moment he realized Gwen was the only woman who could ever possess his heart. "You know what? This has to stop." He didn't have to explain. They damn well knew what he meant. "You two *cannot* force us to do something we have no desire to do."

He looked to Cassandra, who did not glance away when confronted with the truth.

"We're never getting married." James shook his head. "It's bad enough you two…"

Cassandra finished that thought. "…It's bad enough you got me at my lowest, Mother."

Sarah looked as if that were the most damning thing her daughter could have said. "*I was so low you convinced me to steal a man's seed.*" James wanted to believe that such foolishness was a result of a lack of clear thinking. The Cassandra he wanted to remember was a woman who could at least stand by what was morally right. Even if she thought he had signed off on it – and legally, he had – it wasn't the same as her asking him for permission to create his child.

But they could discuss *that* again later.

"I don't think you understand, son," Albert said. "If you think this is only about you and Cassandra, then you are more foolish than I ever thought."

"Then what's it about, Dad?"

The old man narrowed his eyes. "You are my only child. If you think I'm letting you marry a woman who…"

"James," Gwen interrupted, "it's time. I was about to tell them, anyway."

The foyer was silent. A creak on the main staircase announced the ill-timed arrival of Ophelia Merange, bedecked in a navy-blue sleeping gown. James looked to his mother with a grim understanding that she may be shocked to hear the news… that wasn't much news after all.

"Mom," James said in greeting, before turning to his father. "Dad. I insist you understand that I could never marry Cassandra, even if you hauled me to the altar and shoved a pen into my hand." He was impressed that Cassandra did not bristle when he said that. Perhaps she had truly come to understand the situation they were in as well. Maybe he could finally have a friendly relationship with his biggest childhood companion after all. *Maybe*… There was a reason she was one of the only people he ever told.

"Don't you dare." Sarah slapped her purse against her leg when she raced to Albert's side. "Albert, what if they're…"

"I'm already married to Gwen."

James's voice uncharacteristically carried through the wide halls of his childhood home. He had never been a loud speaker. Not the kind of guy who bolstered his ego and presence with a voice nobody asked to hear. Nor had he *yelled* his announcement. But James would be damned if his father didn't hear the truth.

Albert was the only one shocked. And Sarah, although her audible gasp and leering at Gwen was more cartoonish than anything.

"Don't make jokes like that at a time like this," Albert snapped.

"I'm not joking." James marched over and grabbed Gwen's hand. Her eyes widened when she was brought against his side. "Gwen and I married two years ago. We didn't tell anyone, because quite frankly, it wasn't anyone's business."

This wasn't how James wanted his family to find out he was a married man, let alone that it happened beneath their noses. *It was so easy to elope.* A quick trip to another city. A weekend honeymoon and a ceremony wrapped in one. The ink on the marriage license was barely dry before they returned to their everyday lives, with only their secret to bring a little bit of renewed happiness to their days.

It was an act made in passion. When Gwen discovered she would never have children without intervention, James proposed to her. Not because he found her infertility *romantic,* but because he wanted to assuage her fears that he would want to break up now that their lack of children was assured. "*You're the only son in your family,*" she had said through her fearful tears. "*Why would you want someone like me? What if you change your mind about kids? The world won't end if I don't reproduce, but your family might collapse!*"

James and Gwen had never been the type of couple to make a big deal about their relationship. They let their friends go on thinking they were merely cohabitating with, "Eh, we might get married one day," hanging in the air. It helped prevent the rumor from spreading and getting back to the Meranges. It also let them keep living their lives without fanfare, because Gwen had barely survived the adjustment period when she became James's girlfriend, let alone his wife.

They would tell everyone one day. Maybe they would have a proper wedding and act as if that were the day they legally became man and wife, while always keeping the truth to themselves. Or perhaps they would announce it at their thirtieth anniversary party. *I never wanted it to be like this.* Put on the spot and hoping that the truth might deter his own family from ruining his life.

"You didn't have a problem with Gwen for years," James said to his father. "Is it because I'm in my thirties now? Does the thought of me being with the woman I *love* and not the one you've chosen for me threaten you so much?"

Albert continued his scowl. Sarah reached for him. He pulled away, the eternal coward he was. While Sarah had no shame showing him affection in front of his wife, Albert would never reciprocate in front of other people. Honestly, James felt nothing but pity for Lady Welsh.

And his own mother, the woman he thought he would shock the most – yet Ophelia merely looked upon her husband with a knowing glare.

"He's a grown man, Albert," she said. "We should be celebrating the fact he has loved a more than decent woman for so long. We don't need more money." Ophelia opened her mouth again before her husband could interrupt her. "What we need is some *sanity* in this family! Do you know what's insane? You two carrying on like two awestruck teenagers who don't know their lips from their asses!"

Sarah held her hand to her chest. Gwen stifled a chuckle. The fact she could laugh at a time like this only solidified what James loved about her.

"Did you know, Mom?"

"Gwen told me," Ophelia said. "A few weeks ago."

James squeezed his wife's hand. "I told Cassandra a little while ago. So," he said, louder, "she already knew."

"Are you implying that we were the only ones here who didn't know about this?" Albert gestured to the hands held before him. Gwen's faltered within James's, but he did not relent his grip on his wife's fingers. "How could you? How *dare* you do that without informing us?"

"Because it was between us." James wrapped his arm around Gwen's shoulders and held her close to his side. "We decided we didn't want a large affair you would surely demand, assuming you even gave us your blessing. So why have a wedding? Why bring that drama into our lives? I realized that Gwen is the only woman I could ever want to marry. She's perfect for me, and I like to think I'm pretty perfect for her." He didn't wait for Gwen to back him up. "You got what you really wanted, Dad. You got a grandson with the only woman you approved. I've forgiven you for that. Now, forgive me for what I have done. Let me have this." James squeezed his wife. She shuddered against him, and he decided that was her way of saying she loved him. "Let me have Gwen."

Albert spat something about foolish children and their insistence on ruining everything their parents ever built for them. Didn't James know that this went beyond children? This was their reputation! This followed them into the business world! Not everyone was a soft-hearted, lovey-dovey sod who overlooked poor choices in partners. Wasn't it bad enough that everyone and their grandmothers knew where Gwen and James hung out every weekend? That they were sexual deviants who indulged in too much debauchery? Of course Gwen shouldn't have children! Not when half the city had seen her pussy at that club! How could Albert condone a woman like *her* as even the stepmother of his grandchildren?

"Half the city has seen her pussy," Cassandra snapped back at him. "The other half has been in mine, so I fail to see the real difference."

That was what made Sarah faint into Albert's arms. It was also the final word Cassandra imparted upon them before showing herself out the door, with hardly a word to James or anyone's mother.

Gwen soon followed her. At first, James assumed his wife had burst from his hold to go after Cassandra and say something to her. But when she blew past Cassandra's car and made a break for the front gate, James knew that something was terribly wrong.

If he didn't move quickly, that might be the last he ever saw of the woman he married.

CHAPTER 13

GWEN

The trip home was a complete blur. Gwen hailed a ride share as soon as she was off the Merange's property, her feet already sore and her heart pumping in her chest.

Everything had been too much. Between the invasive interrogation – and subsequent pay-off – at the hands of Albert and Sarah, Gwen had not been prepared to have her marriage revealed in front of so many people. *James told Cassandra! When the hell did he do that?* It was totally different from Gwen telling Ophelia about the marriage. That had been protecting herself in front of her mother-in-law. Ophelia was the only ally she had. Cassandra was…

Cassandra was a part of the problem!

Gwen didn't care if James would never marry the mother of his child, let alone lust after her. That wasn't the point. *Okay, it was, a little bit.* But simply believing him wasn't enough. Cassandra represented everything that was toxic in that world. Men of power and money such as Albert Merange were not above stealing their own son's sperm if it meant getting the grandchild of his dreams. Timing said that the plan was hatched as soon as Gwen discovered she was as good as infertile. Albert wasn't taking his chances.

It was also right when she married James, not that his family had known about that. At least *that* hadn't leaked!

I don't even think about being married. My view of James never changed. Signing a piece of paper and saying a few words in front of an officiant wasn't romantic. Gwen wasn't a wedding type of woman, and James had agreed he would only go along with a big wedding if it was what she really wanted. He had been as happy to elope with her and go on a lovely weekend vacation. (The real "honeymoon" came a month later, when he could take more time off work and she finished the travel plans.) The weekend trip was the most romantic part. Dinner by the sea. Walks on the beach. Watching the sun set from their suite. Making love after getting out of the hot tub. Waking up to breakfast by the windows.

But it was the same ol' thing, in a good way. Nothing really changed, other than taxes and signing other papers that gave Gwen more rights as James's wife. If anything, being married gave her more relief. She didn't worry about medical matters or inheritance. James would have always made sure she was taken care of, but having that piece of paper meant everything was much more streamlined. The feelings between them didn't change. Gwen didn't think their relationship was stronger or more assured since they married. The only thing that caused the change was *the baby.*

The baby… and what it meant about the family she had married into.

Gwen almost knocked over Rebecca when she burst through her front door. Rebecca asked if everything was all right, but Gwen had a one-track mind that led her upstairs to the master suite.

She pulled out a suitcase and began the deranged process of throwing in whatever clothing she thought she might need. Where was she going? *I don't know. A hotel. My parents' place. Anywhere I can be alone and figure things out.* Her flight or fight response had kicked in again, this time with the full force of a family that wanted her out.

Gwen didn't belong with these people. She never had. Everything, from the gilded house to the fun nights on the town, had merely been a long, meandering escape. She had been Alice in Wonderland. Now it was time to return to England with only faint memories of Red Queens and Mad Hatters.

We should have never married. That had been the catalyst for all the shit. Maybe the dream could have continued if they never brought that into their lives. Or maybe it would have made it easier to leave when shit hit the fan.

Gwen didn't know if she wanted a separation, a divorce, or *what.* All she knew was that she wanted to get away. Possibly forever. At least for a month or a year.

Forever sounded good.

She hadn't packed quickly enough, however. Not when James had his own car and must have followed her the moment she bailed on the Meranges. There was no doubt he would come after her, because he was James, and he probably would have followed her to Siberia if that's where she was hellbent on fleeing.

Gwen dropped the shirt in her hand and held back a frustrated sob. She braced against the end of the bed the moment James leaped into their suite, her name on his lips.

She didn't respond.

"Gwen…" James kept his distance. "What's going on? What are you doing?"

She slammed the top of her suitcase shut. *I don't know what I put in there. Underwear? Jeans?* She didn't care. The only reason she packed anything at all was because she barely had enough rationalization rattling around her brain to realize she needed clean underwear wherever she went. Besides, throwing clothes into a suitcase and *slamming it shut* was so satisfying.

"What does it look like I'm doing?" she asked her husband. "I'm leaving."

Even though she didn't look at him, Gwen sensed the panic emanating from James's body. "*What?*" He came closer, but Gwen must have thrown up so many barriers that he smacked his head against every one of her defenses – he practically crumpled on the floor, disbelief consuming the air. "No… Gwen…"

The crack in his voice gutted her. Gwen pulled her suitcase off the bed and finally turned toward James, her tearful eyes meeting the sorrow in his. "I'm sorry," she said. "I can't do this. I thought I could. I wouldn't have married you if I didn't think it would be forever, but… I can't."

He blocked the only way out of the suite. *Don't make this harder, James. Please.* Gwen needed a clear getaway. An escape. A way out that wouldn't pull her heart even farther up her throat than it already was. *Accept it, James. It was never meant to be for so long.*

"Because of my family?" He held his opened hands out to her. "They don't matter! There's nothing they can do to us! What's the worst my father could do, huh? Cut me out of his will and make everything go to Patrick? He wouldn't dare. He needs me to run the company!"

Bottom lip trembling, Gwen unleashed the exasperation consuming her tired soul. "You know it's not merely that! How could you suggest that the worst thing that could happen is *you* being cut out of the will? Don't you get it?" She clasped her hands against her face. How could she save that face, though, when the tears refused to stop? "They'll always go after *me*! Your father's plan was to drive me away! Well!" Gwen lowered one wet hand and allowed her husband to see the full effect of his father's actions. "It worked! You stubborn-ass Merange losers always get your fucking ways! You get me for a little while, and your dad gets rid of me!"

The tension melted out of James's shoulders as if that was enough to kill him.

"I love you," he muttered in defeat. "Isn't that enough?"

That was a blow unlike Gwen had ever experienced. Yet she still said, "Not always."

James held his hand to his face. Gwen had cried enough already to know what went through her husband's head, and how it threatened to make him the most vulnerable she had ever seen him. While James had cried in front of her before, it wasn't an everyday occurrence. Even a softie like him had ingested his father's warnings about masculinity and devoured what his frat and his friends said about *tears are for girls.* To see him cry was on par with ripping his heart out and squeezing it in his hand for her to behold.

"It's not just one thing, James," Gwen attempted to explain. "It's not only the kid that came out of nowhere, or the overbearing father who hates my guts, or the other woman everyone thinks you should be with instead of me… if it were *just* one of those things, I could survive. I could even be happy, knowing that you've got my back and won't let them touch me. But…" She sighed. "It's not just one of those things. It's all of them. It's everything else they might try to do to get their perfect vision of paradise. The people in your family are a bunch of broken fucks, and they've got enough clout to make it worse for themselves… and for us."

"You think I don't know that?" James asked through a pinch to his nose. His eyes remained squeezed shut. One hand slammed against his hip while the other shook something off its fingers. The man needed a gold medal in holding back tears. "I grew up in that family! They're messed up even by society's standards. Jesus!" He turned away. There must have been tears on his cheeks. "I don't agree with a single thing they've done. It was disgusting of my father to offer you money to leave me. He's a delusional ass who thinks I'll fall in line if I think I have no other choice." James shirked his jacket and tossed it onto the floor. Gwen sat on the edge of their bed, crestfallen. "He doesn't understand that this isn't 1980 anymore. This isn't the '50s of my grandfather's years. It's not the Victorian age. For God's sake… he's so furious that I might get to be with the woman I love, and this is what he does?"

Gwen shook her head. "His would-be wife suggested that you would be so heartbroken that Cassandra would have no issue sweeping in and cheering you right up."

"That is the most insulting thing I have ever heard, and I've heard quite a bit of insults these past couple of years. You can't be serious if you think everything he'll try is all about getting to you."

"It is, though!" Why couldn't he see that? Gwen wasn't making it up! She wasn't trying to make herself into the ultimate victim! God knew she had tried to power through the bullshit over the past several years. Being with James meant giving up much of her old life in favor of one she barely recognized. Assimilating herself into high society, making friends with heiresses and other up-and-coming women such as herself, and adjusting to a life where she never had to settle on a career or even *work* had taken a toll on her mental (and sometimes physical) health. The payoff hadn't only been the money, or knowing that her parents were taken care of should her dad have another heart attack. It was being with James. The man who had stolen her heart and offered her everything she could ever want, both inside their home and out of it.

He had opened her eyes to pleasures she never even knew she desired. He had spoiled her so much that she sometimes felt like a flashy princess having her fun before going home when the summer's over. He had been by her side when her father had his first heart attack. He promised to be there no matter what happened to her or her family.

Gwen loved him, dearly. But was that enough to put up with what his family conspired? For fuck's sake, they put his baby in another woman!

Ah, that was it, wasn't it? That would always be the kicker that brought more tears.

James sat down next to her as she cried in earnest. Gwen didn't look to him for comfort, but she didn't push him away, either. She wanted to kiss him. She wanted to scream at him.

She wanted this all to go away.

"What's really wrong, Gwenny?" James placed his hand softly on the small of her back. Shudders of love claimed Gwen's body.

It still wasn't enough.

"Talk to me. Please."

She sniffed the last of her awkward tears. Snot stained her sleeve. "I feel so powerless in your family. They get whatever they want. They heard I couldn't have kids, and they went out and took advantage of your friend's mental health to knock her up with their precious heir."

"Listen to me, Gwenny." James's hand tightened on her shoulder. He didn't turn her around, but she knew he wanted to. "You're right that my family thinks they have all this power. They get away with a lot of shit, too. But *you* are not powerless, and you never have been. Now more than ever, though, you hold all the cards. My parents will wither away." He choked at the thought. What son wanted to admit that? "But we will be around much longer. You are my wife. Maybe it's time we finally talk about what that means."

Gwen turned her whole body away from him. It had taken her months to finally warm up to the idea of James being her *husband.* They had always called each other partners from the moment they moved in together. Husband, wife… those words didn't change a thing between them. Their lives went on as usual.

Until the baby, anyway.

"The first time I saw you," James continued, his voice strained and soft. "I knew you would probably be my wife one day."

"You've told me that before." The day they eloped. It had been incredibly romantic back then. Now? James played cards he had no business playing.

"I'll keep telling you that, because it's true. I'd gone out with a million women before you, but the moment I saw you, I wondered what it would be like to finally find that one woman who changed my life forever. After our first date, I knew it was meant to be. I only hoped you thought the same thing."

I had wanted it to be true… Butterflies fluttered in Gwen's body after their first date at the planetarium. She hadn't known what to expect after hooking up with the man in the back of her place of work. *I was prepared for anything, like some friends with benefits situation. I never expected him to be… more…* They had gone back to James's place that night. Made love for what felt like *hours.* Yet the man had been so courteous and giddy in her presence, that Gwen couldn't help but feel that this was the romance she didn't know she had been waiting for.

Then they moved in together.

Then they got married without telling a soul. Like so much else in their relationship, it had been something for them. Perhaps they couldn't hide them living together. But if they could have? Gwen doubted she would have ever mentioned it. The strength of her relationship with James wasn't anyone else's business. The whole point of getting married – in secret, no less – was to protect themselves. And to assert how much they intended to be together.

Forever.

"Nobody will ever take away from you being my other half." James took her hand and held it in his lap. "Not even I could do that. It would be like denying the other part of my soul."

Gwen opened her mouth to say something, but the words refused to come out. She wanted to agree with her husband that they were two halves of one mighty whole. Perhaps they were perfectly fine on their own, and God knew other people didn't need to enjoy them as a unit to know their worth and what they uniquely brought to the world. But they were strongest and happiest when together. The hardest part about leaving James would be that void left behind.

Not the money. Not the trips around the world. The man himself. That's all Gwen wanted.

Too bad, like most trips around the world, he came with so much *baggage*. Too bad she had some baggage of her own. Both conflated with each other.

"Fuck…" Gwen wiped a tear from her eye before doubling over into a mess of sobs.

James wrapped both arms around her, bringing her closer to his chest and blowing a breath of assurance over her ear. Once upon a time, that would have been enough to soothe her soul. *It was the only thing that brought me a little calm when my father was sick.* Gwen had been a daddy's girl. Almost losing her father to a heart attack had made her comatose for more than a few days. How could one woman hold so much grief for a man who hadn't actually *died?*

Was that why she cried now? Grief?

I'm acting like I lost a baby or something… The life event that could have either permanently split them apart or made them stronger together. If something like that happened, Gwen didn't doubt that she and James would be inseparable. And, she knew, she would be the one to get over it first. James would be devastated. Because he was the man who would have loved children, even if he told her he didn't need them to be happy with her.

God. That killed her more than anything.

"They're right!" She pulled herself from his hold and sprinted halfway across the room. Where was she going? *Nowhere.* Not in that direction. A large window. Curtains rustling in the breeze that came through a slit in the bottom pane. An antique lamp that was sometimes the only thing on when they made love in the middle of the night. Almost a decade's worth of love, and they were still sometimes too shy to have sex in a brightly lit room. "I don't fit into your family, James. That's the issue here. I don't fit into your f*amily.* You and I may be great when we're alone, but when you combine those people… did you know that our parents have never met before? My mom is always asking when we're going to have Thanksgiving or Christmas with the Meranges. What if she finds out we're married, and they still don't know my in-laws? The only reason I haven't tried to set something up is because of your father! I couldn't bear it if he insulted my parents to their faces."

"You know I've offered to have my mother at least meet them…"

That would only work because your mother doesn't have the spine to insult them. Gwen wasn't delusional. Ophelia was so coddled in her lifestyle that lower middle-class people like the Mitchells would have made her clutch her vintage pearls. All it would take was Gwen's father belching at the dinner table or her mother asking what department store the crystal came from. Ophelia may not say anything, but Gwen knew that woman well enough by now to read the shock and appellation on a parasol-shielded countenance.

Besides, who was she kidding? Sarah Welsh would probably introduce herself as James's mother before Ophelia had the chance.

It was bad enough her parents knew about Patrick. Gwen's mother was still convinced that James had cheated. She couldn't wrap her mind around a whole family conspiring to steal a man's sperm.

"Your family is toxic, James. They've been poisoning us for years. Yes, even your mother." Gwen grabbed a tissue from the vanity and wiped her face. She didn't bother to blow her nose. More snot was coming, anyway. "Until a year ago, she kept pressing me about kids. You know how she is. She would never outright say, '*Where are my grandbabies, you slut?*' Her MO is to be sooo passive-aggressive that I choke." Gwen would never forget the day, three years ago, when Ophelia invited her tea at the Merange's estate and grilled her about her familial potential. That was before Gwen had a firm diagnosis. To think, a woman could be so comfortable in her infertility, yet all it took was one asinine comment…

Gwen wished that James hadn't stood up.

"I'm never going to give you children." Gwen held her hand around her throat. "Honestly? I never wanted to. Maybe if it were an accident… but you know I'm not the type to stop taking my birth control and hope my disorders let me get pregnant." She also didn't want to start all those blasted treatments for the slim chance. What kind of life was that? Maybe some women were game to play Russian Roulette, but Gwen didn't have the *drive* and desire. She'd rather spend her years cuddling up next to James and living every moment as it came. *Why would I put myself through that if it wasn't what I even wanted?*

"That's *fine,* Gwen!" James held his hands out to her. Helpless. Lost. He didn't know what to say, and he didn't know what to do for her. Gwen hated seeing him like this. "I've told you! Even before we found out about… anything… I told you I didn't care if we didn't have kids! Not like it's some brand-new trend! Plenty of other people will have plenty of kids to populate this planet!"

"I don't care about other people." Gwen couldn't believe she was sharing this. "I care that the choice was ripped from my life. First I don't even get to choose whether or not I have kids… and then…" She swallowed. "Oh, look, another woman had your baby anyway."

James shook his head. "I knew this started around that time, Gwenny, but… I had no say in that, either."

"No. But your family saw something they wanted, and they got it. What else will they do? How will they continue to break us apart? How will they keep pushing me aside until I no longer exist in your life? I need to leave now. If I do, then I have a chance at taking charge of at least one thing in my life with you."

He didn't say anything. At first, Gwen assumed she had left him flummoxed. For once, the chatty James Merange had no words.

There was a little power for her in that situation. Not enough, but a little.

No. James hadn't been left speechless. He knew exactly what to say, and Gwen saw it when he bridged the small gap between them in their bedroom. *The place we've called ours for so long. The place I think of as my home. With you, James.* Here came the tears again.

"You still think of it as your life with me." James gently placed both hands on her shoulders. "Do you *really* want to leave, Gwen? Is that what you want? Because if that's what you *really* want, I'll let you go. I won't stop you from doing what you need to do. But if you give me even the slightest hint that you're not interested in leaving, I will fight for you until the day I die. I honest to God do not believe that we'll be happier apart than we are together, even with all the crap my family puts us through."

Gwen's lip trembled. That was all the answer he needed to come over and embrace her.

"I love you, Gwenny." James buried his face in the crook of her neck. She wrapped her arms around his shoulders and held on for her life. "I know it's been hard. A lot has happened since we met, let alone in the past year. But it *will* get better. My family knows that you're my wife now. They can't take what we have away from us. Now, and forever."

"But…"

"No buts, Gwen." He stroked her hair before pulling it to the side and grazing his nose against the back of her neck. The scintillating sensation made her hold herself closer to him. Her lover. Her protector.

Her husband.

"I love you. You're the only woman I've ever *loved,* and if I lost you, there could never be another woman in my heart again. I know this. You know this. Even if I married someone else in the far-off future, it wouldn't be real love."

She snorted. "You're such a romantic."

"Admit it. It's why you fell in love with me."

No… I fell in love with you for so many other reasons. "I love you, James."

"Then don't leave me. Not when we know it will destroy us."

"I just…" Gwen still couldn't believe that this would work. Even if they packed their bags and moved to Nepal, the Meranges would continue getting their way back home. *It would be like admitting defeat. A consolation prize.* Gwen wanted to live her life the way she deserved. Openly. Firmly. Without prejudice, toward herself and from others. "You've got this whole other life beyond me now. What do I do when you're off being a dad? What's going to happen if they do it again? What if I…" Gwen swallowed, her hands gently pushing her away from her husband. "What if I want to become a part of the bigger picture one day, and I'm shut out? Do I become the ghost-wife floating in the background? Who *am* I to that little boy?" The kid didn't know how good he had it right now. He had no idea what his family had done. One day, when he was old enough to understand, he'd be appalled. Patrick may not be Gwen's son, but she'd be damned if he didn't have the right support network to weather that clusterfuck. Losing that support might mean he turned out even worse than the family members tearing him down for their own gain. One good dad wasn't enough to counteract the diabolical grandparents and a mother who was as spineless as Ophelia.

"Gwen… the only person keeping you away from Patrick is *you*." James cupped her chin with his fingers and offered her a kiss. She wasn't yet ready to take it. "I've hoped for a long time now that you would be more than my wife. If I had a child out there, I hoped you would be his mother too."

"But Cassandra is his…"

"She and I have talked countless times about this. She agrees that there is no issue with you being Patrick's active stepmother, if that's what you want. Or you could be his second mother. It's up to *you,* and whatever relationship you form with him. You can be as much of a parent as you want."

Gwen looked away. Her hands wrung together. "I don't know if I could do that. There's so many damned *feelings* with him…"

"I've always wanted you to take your time with him. I know it's been a shock. God knows I do, Gwen. Like that, I was a dad, and I had no say in it. But that means you saw me become a dad when we had just married. You had me all to yourself, then you didn't."

She couldn't help but laugh. "You stole that from the therapist, didn't you?"

James matched her smile, yet he said, "Maybe we should go back to the counselor. With a new attitude. A new united front. I admit, the thought of tackling this by ourselves is daunting." He scratched the back of his head. "Maybe the counselor could help us figure out what to do. No shame in it, right?"

No, but Gwen hadn't been ready the last time they went to the couple's counselor. She had always been on the defensive. Ready to blow up if she felt even slightly… slighted. It hadn't taken much that past year. Finding out what the Meranges and Welshes had done was like being punched in the face. It was the greatest insult. Greater than them offering her cash to leave.

"I'd be embarrassed."

"I know." At least he didn't try to tell her she had no reason to be embarrassed, even if that was what he believed! James wasn't the kind of man to convince her she didn't feel what she genuinely experienced, though. *He's too good for me. What have I ever done to deserve a great guy like him?* "But it's like anything else. Eventually, you'll get over the embarrassment and things simply… are."

Gwen briefly met his eyes again. "Did you feel embarrassed when you first started meeting your son?"

"Embarrassed, ashamed, angry… I can't even explain what exactly I felt. It was like all three of those at once. But the beauty is that he's so young right now that the only thing he understands is that I'm a man he can trust. I'm his dad. Honestly, the only reason I don't visit him more often is because I was afraid that you resented me for it."

"I'm also guessing the Welshes limit your contact."

"Cassandra and I have an understanding that he is my son and I can see him whenever I want. Within reason, obviously. I prefer that arrangement to having to sue her for custody. My lawyer has assured me I have an easy case to win with all the evidence I have. Not like any of them have denied anything."

"I still don't know." Gwen lowered her finger when she realized she was gnawing on her knuckle. A nervous habit she thought she kicked years ago. "I never saw myself as a mother. But after I got with you, I assumed that meant you would never be a father. How can you be a parent, but I'm not?"

"Gwenny," James said with his replenishing reserves of reassurances, "you can literally be whatever you want. Be an only-goes-to-birthday-parties-and-graduations stepmom. Be a cool aunt. Spend time with him alone or only when I'm around. I'm not asking you to love my son. I'm asking you to support me, and to support him."

James had touched on the last thing often keeping Gwen up at night. "But what if I do end up loving him? What if he makes me realize I want my own children?" The tears came back. "What do I do then?"

"*We,* Gwenny. You're asking what *we* would do. Because the moment you want something, I'm going to make sure it happens."

"Your son is going to be so spoiled."

"Hey, it's different with a kid. I think. Still sorting that one out."

Gwen took her husband's hands. "I don't know what's going to happen. Used to be that I loved not knowing what our future held. The spontaneity made me happy. Now I'm not so sure."

"Falling in love with you was the most spontaneous thing to ever happen to me. It will be difficult for anything to top that, including having kids come at us out of nowhere." He touched the tip of her nose. "I guarantee there will be no more surprise babies, though. Surprise pregnancies, maybe…"

"If there are surprise pregnancies, they better be *mine.*"

"Let me tell you how I've spent the past year locking down my frozen sperm." James adopted a wistful look as he grinned at the window behind Gwen. "I'm saving it all for you. All my sperm, both new and old."

Gwen cringed. That was the exact reaction he was looking for, wasn't it? *Never change, James.* "Just keep the old sperm out of your family's hands, thanks."

He turned his head back toward hers and opened his arms wide. "You're my wife. Nobody but you could ever change that. And that means you are the most important person in my world." James's caress preempted his kiss to her lips. "I love you, Gwenny. Be my wife, forever. We'll make up what that means as we go along."

"Because that's been working so well so far," she muttered.

"Do you love me, Gwen?"

She sighed. "I must love you if I'm about to unpack that suitcase…"

"And?"

She matched his grin. "And demand that you take me somewhere fun. Right now."

"Las Vegas it is!"

"I was thinking the club or the planetarium, but Vegas is fun too."

"Right. Club. Planetarium." James snapped his fingers. "Planetarium, then the club? Vegas as soon as we can swing it?"

"I don't think the planetarium would appreciate me walking in wearing nothing but a skimpy dress and not much else."

"Why, Gwenyth," James said with a waggle of his eyebrows. "What do you have in mind for this club experience that requires you to be half naked?"

She pressed her hands against his chest, reveling in the strength, devotion, and vitality rumbling beneath his skin. "Take me to the club and make sure half the town knows that I'm the only woman you worship."

Yup. She still had it. The ability to make him hard with one string of words, that is.

"I don't think the club is ready for that."

"*I'm* ready for that." Gwen brushed her knuckles against his cheeks. "If you're also ready, let's do it."

"Been ready since the moment I met you."

Gwen threaded her arm with his. "Somehow, I had known that."

"Kinda hard to hide how much I love you."

She squeezed his hand. "Prove it."

Eventually, James would realize proving such devotion was a daily occurrence for the rest of his life. Until then, Gwen would enjoy the look on his face every time she asked for his proof of love.

SEVEN YEARS AGO

Part 3

The car pulled up to a gated property on the far edge of town. Gwen had driven past this affluent division of the city plenty of times, but had never slowed down to give it a hearty look. Why would she, when she always assumed she would never, ever have anything to do with it? The large mansions with intricate landscaping, gated security, and bus stops built and serviced solely for "servants'" use was the stuff of ridiculous daytime TV. Gwen never thought in a million years that she would have anything to do with one of these manors, most of them built a hundred years ago. Some of them had been the homes of more than one family. Others, like the Meranges', were built to the eternal tastes of the patrilineal people who inhabited them.

Her eyes rolled back as she vainly attempted to take in the sweeping maple trees bristling in the breeze. It was easier than noticing the details on the gothic fountain or deciphering what dialect of Spanish the landscapers spoke as they tore out an old rose bush and replaced it with a sure-to-be-spectacular rhododendron bush.

To think, it was a cloudy, humid day, and Gwen was still awestruck by the grandeur of James' childhood home.

Until that day, she had only visited his two-bedroom apartment downtown. Granted, that place was luxury-and-a-half, as befitting a young man of old money means, but Gwen didn't think it could get more ridiculous than an on-call maid or a chef who made the rounds at every apartment to make sure everyone's refrigerators were stocked and then food prepped for dinner. James had been *so* p*roud* when he made Gwen dinner for the third date together. It wasn't until she visited him during the day that she discovered those spaghetti and meatballs were prepped by an Italian chef. All James did was cook the noodles, heat up the sauce, and throw it all together. *Also explained how the meatballs were slightly cold.* Gwen had loved it anyway, because James had been *so proud,* and she was convinced she was falling in love with him.

She wondered how far that love extended when facing the truth of his heritage.

"Ready?" James had parked his car next to a Rolls-Royce. The vanity plate said *MERANGE* in giant letters that suggested its owner wanted everyone in town to know his name before recognizing his car. *Oh my God, it's his father, isn't it?* According to James, his father was the reason she hadn't met his parents yet. They had been dating for over six months, and were only a few weeks shy of the anniversary of the first time they met. Rarely had James mentioned his parents, even though they lived in town.

Now Gwen knew why.

Everything, from the gothic façade of the manor to the uniformed housekeepers having a smoke break on the other side of a small entrance, were nothing like the image Gwen had built of her boyfriend. His wit, good-naturedness, and charisma were what pulled her into his gravity. The tender way he kissed her before fucking her hard and his romantic sensibilities he displayed while they visited local sex clubs kept her by his side.

None of that was broadcasted by his childhood home. Perhaps Gwen merely had butterflies in her stomach, but this did not bode well.

She also felt woefully underdressed in her green sundress and strappy brown sandals. James had said she looked "perfect" when he picked her up, but she hadn't failed to notice his three-piece suit and the five-thousand dollar watch on his wrist. He only wore that when he had to see his father. *It must be a Christmas present.* James usually kept the more expensive and ostentatious accessories at home when he didn't do much more than go on dates with Gwen or hang out with his college friends.

Both doors of the car opened. Gwen hesitated before stepping out, the heels of her sandals tapping gently against the paved driveway. James rounded the back of his car and offered to take her hand. "Can you believe it?" He grinned as he led her to the front steps of the impressive manor. "Hardly a thing's been changed since it was built in 1913. One year before the first great war. My great-grandfather considered himself a lucky bastard he finished building this thing before wars broke out."

"Did you meet your great-grandfather?"

"Hell, no. My father's the first man in the family to not kill himself by sixty." When Gwen gave him an exasperated look, he explained, "I don't mean they literally killed themselves, Gwenny. They had shitastic lifestyles."

"So does that make your dad a teetotaler and not a fan of adrenaline?"

"Eschewing adrenaline, yes. Teetotaling? Hardly." James left it at that as he hauled Gwen toward the gilded front doors.

Did his mother meet them there? No. They were greeted by a butler in coat and tails, who warmly greeted James and shot Gwen a devil-may-care look.

Really. The devil couldn't care.

"Mr. Merange is awaiting you and Ms. Mitchell in the salon. He's asked me to escort you there upon your admittance."

"The salon, huh?" James's hold on Gwen's hand faltered. "Where's Mom?"

"Lady Merange has been held up at the country club, due to the road closure on the highway." The butler stopped before a closed door. "She assures me that she will be home in time to meet Ms. Mitchell, and apologizes that she couldn't return in time for your appointment."

Appointment? This man has to make an appointment to see his parents? That was a level of absurdity Gwen had never heard of before. Besides, James had said his mother had barely worked in her life, and his father only attended a few business meetings these days. He was still in charge of the family company and fortune, but most of the decisions were made by a board, and James was the chief charismatic schmoozer.

"All right." James said that, yet the look on his face implied he wasn't sure he wanted to enter the salon. "Let's go meet my dad, Gwen."

She braced herself as the door opened. Everything James had ever said about his father, Albert Merange, made her think of a man steeped in sophistication to the point he had never seen a real department store in his life. The man had been in one of the most exclusive fraternities in the country, had gone to a prestigious New England boarding school, and spent so much of his life either holed up in his manor or jet setting to *other* manors around the world. *How can I compete with that?* Gwen was from a town so small that the richest family claimed a McMansion with a dock overlooking the local lake. *That* was high living, and the wife still worked as a local bank manager, and the husband compensated his construction job with paid fishing excursions. Gwen had been good friends with their daughter in seventh grade. That birthday party, with the hired Pearl Jam cover band and tiered cake from the bakery one town over, was the most decadent thing Gwen Mitchell had ever seen.

Until now.

She instantly recognized Albert. Not based on any pictures James had shared of him, but from the bright, insidious look in his aged eyes. His salt and pepper hair was perfectly combed so no spot had too much salt or too much pepper. His chiseled jaw made him more imposing than the police officer who once pulled Gwen over for speeding. A bespoke suit made of fine Italian fabric made Gwen itch in her department store dress.

That was what intimidated her before the man spoke.

"Son." Albert stood with the grace of a well-trained greyhound. *My God. Where did that comparison come from? Have I ever seen any greyhounds in my life, let alone* well-trained *ones?* "So good to see you. You're looking quite well." They shook hands and exchanged identical grins. When Albert turned to the tall blonde woman in a green sundress, however, he lost half of his smile. It wasn't a lecherous look greeting her, but *highly* critical, as if he surmised her ability to give him grandchildren or embarrass him at high-society functions with one look…

…and had found her wanting.

"Dad." James put his arm around Gwen, forcing one of her feet forward and her hand out to clutch Albert's. "This is my girlfriend, Gwenyth. You know, the one I can't stop talking about?" His grin was one of pure joy and love. The careful smile on Albert's visage, however, remained critical of the woman before him.

"Gwenyth. How lovely to meet you." Albert offered her a curt shake of the hand before pulling his away. "Is that a Welsh name?"

"It is, I believe." *Really. The first thing I say to him is clarifying if my name is Welsh?* "Pleasure to meet you, sir."

"Different spelling from the actress, though," James said. "But we all call her Gwen."

"Yes, I insist that you call me Gwen, sir."

Albert said nothing, let alone any variation of her name.

They had settled at the table overlooking the gardens when a servant entered with a platter of coffees and light finger-snacks. He also carried with him a message.

"Lady and Ms. Welsh are here, sir."

James did a double-take; Albert remained content. Gwen, meanwhile, had no idea what any of that meant. Was that code about her and her name?

If only.

"They must be dropping by for a quick chat." Albert shrugged. "Show them in. I'm sure Cassandra would love to chat with her old friend."

James was still speechless. When he turned to Gwen, she offered a shrug like Albert's and a wan smile that suggested she was fine with anything.

Two minutes later, an older woman and her grown daughter entered the salon, the both bedecked in matching wrap-dresses that highlighted the older woman's flawless skin and the younger woman's bouncing curls. Cassandra, the young woman, took a step back when she saw James and Gwen. Her mother went straight to

Albert and shared with him a look that Gwen instantly realized was one of love.

She should have listened to her gut when it said that none of these people would be good for her.

CHAPTER 14

GWEN

Rebecca informed Gwen that her guest had arrived. Too bad Gwen was in the middle of piercing her ear with a gem she hadn't worn in years.

"Ow! Shit!" Gwen searched for a tissue to fend any blood off at the pass. The earring dropped to the vanity and almost bounced to the floor, where it would undoubtedly disappear, possibly to never be seen again.

So much for that.

Rebecca double-backed to make sure her employer was all right before going downstairs to tend to the guest. After ensuring that she wouldn't bleed all over her dress, Gwen combed a few errant hairs and slipped into her Miu Miu patent leather pumps she picked up while in Vegas with James. The opulent, multicolored crystals were meant to complement the little black dress on her body. She also wore them because she liked showing them off to other women. Particularly, women people perceived her to have a rivalry with.

Too bad the shoes made her trip halfway down the stairs into the receiving room.

Rebecca met her in the front hall. "Should I bring the cider?"

"Yes. Bring the sampler, if you would." Gwen had no idea if her guest liked particular flavors of cider. She had only heard that a certain someone preferred ciders to other alcoholic infusions. "Is she seated in the receiving room?"

"Yes, ma'am." Rebecca briefly nodded before heading to the kitchen to grab that sampler.

Gwen checked her appearance in the hallway mirror before standing tall on her way into the receiving room. Her guest immediately turned around in her seat.

"So glad you could make it." Gwen extended her fingers to Cassandra, who touched them with her own fingertips and offered a ladylike smile. "And, uh…"

The little boy, dressed in a black T-shirt and a pair of toddler-sized pants, played with a toy on the floor. He glanced up at Gwen with big blue eyes and waved a chubby hand in her direction.

"Patrick is very friendly with strangers." Cassandra did not hurry to pick up her son. *The hell do I do?* She had a feeling Cassandra would bring her son with her, but wasn't expecting a free-range toddler and his small bag of toys.

Sometimes, staring into the face of her husband's son was too much for Gwen to bear. It had been exceptionally difficult before she decided to be a positive presence in her stepson's life. Now it was… *strange.*

"Don't mind him, please." Cassandra motioned for the other empty chair at the small table. "If you try to interrupt him, he might cry. Such a sensitive boy."

Gwen slowly sank into her chair. Rebecca entered, carrying the tray of ciders for them to sample and enjoy. "Must take after his father. Take away James's toys, and he cries too." Gwen didn't mean the video games or pool tables. The man also did not appreciate misplacing his sex swings and dildos.

"The strangers thing is definitely from his father." Cassandra straightened her body-hugging dress. One would think the weather had turned too warm for her to favor those dark colors and long sleeves, but one thing people could say about Cassandra Welsh was that she appreciated a *look*. And she was the master of the long-sleeved body-con dress. "Can't stand them, myself. I shudder to think of what it will be like when Patrick is old enough to invite a plethora of friends over on a daily basis. Because he will."

"I'm assuming those friends will be coming over here, then." Gwen forced a smile. Not because she didn't *feel* friendly, but because this was still new, unknown territory for her. She barely knew how to act around children, let alone how to handle them. *Maybe this was a mistake. I'm not cut out to be a cool aunt or a semi-involved stepmother.* But she had made a promise, both to herself and to her husband, to do her best. James said that she would get over her embarrassment. Well, what if she didn't feel embarrassment now? What if it was pure horror?

Honestly, they were the same thing.

"James is looking forward to playdates and sleepovers," Gwen said. "He's already hired a contractor to remodel Patrick's future room here. I'm sure the blueprints include hidden compartments and secret passages."

Cassandra offered a genuine smile when Gwen's faltered. "There are a lot of old compartments hiding in the Merange house, as you may or may not know. He used to hide in them and scare me when I walked by. I'm *sure* our son has inherited that."

"*Our son.*" Fuck Gwen, because that still hurt to hear. "I'm sure Patrick will enjoy what James has planned. He'll also have plenty of privacy here. He'll be living closer to the help than to our room." That was fortunate for many reasons. Gwen wanted space, and she was sure that a growing boy did as well. Still, what Cassandra did only drove home how different her role would be in Patrick Welsh's life.

"Forgive me," Cassandra said as soon as she caught Gwen's discomfort. "I know how awkward this must be for you. But I appreciate you wanting to get to know our son more. It's important to me that he has family beyond my own. You know how they can be." She looked away when she said that. "I also want to formally apologize for what happened. I know I've apologized before, but I want to do it again. I'll keep apologizing too. Even if you don't want me to, because like with a lot of things, I can't help myself."

Gwen pondered that. *What can't you help yourself with, Cassandra?* Gwen had heard the rumors through the grapevine *and* from James's own mouth. Before the drama happened, he had spent more than a few nights expressing his worries about his old childhood friend. Not only her promiscuity, but her apparent depression, her perilous relationship with her family, and how much of a pushover she had been before a baby. *I'm one of the first to admit that she's changed for the better since becoming a mother… but did it have to be my stepson she had?*

"What's done is done." Gwen swallowed her old thoughts and sat up straight in her chair. This was her home. This was her domain. Her *queendom.* Cassandra was a guest, and not even stirring the pot. Gwen held all the cards in her own home. She directed the mood, the tone, even the topics of discussion. She had to remind herself that. She could run down to the courthouse and legally make her name Mrs. Merange whenever she wanted. "I don't want to dwell on what happened. My goal is to move forward with my husband," she let the word sink in, both for herself, and for the woman sitting across from her, "and do what needs to be done to have a stable family. I'm more inclined to worry about your families and their infuriating ways."

Cassandra sighed. "My mother is a piece of work. So is your father-in-law. It's taken me a long time to realize how reprehensible their behavior has been. When my mother originally approached me about having a baby, I didn't question it. It was like I had been *waiting* for her to suggest something as outlandish as purposely having a baby out of wedlock. By the time I came around to the idea, I didn't even blink when she told me that James had 'agreed' to let me use his sperm. The only thing that shocked me was finding out that he didn't know about it, but by then it was too late. It was my guilt that brought you into this."

"We would've found out eventually." As Patrick grew older, he would look more and more like a Merange. The rumor mill would pump out a million stories about a clandestine affair between the second generation of Meranges and Welshes. Honestly, that would've been worse. At least this way Gwen could help control the story that unraveled in the years to come. Someone had to keep those PR agencies in business, after all. "I appreciate your apology."

Cassandra said something to her son before lifting her shoulders back and offering Gwen a steady gaze. *Not used to looking her in the eye.* How sad was that? But Gwen assumed that was another sign of Cassandra gradually reclaiming her sense of self outside of her toxic family.

They would never be close friends, but Gwen was determined to be cordial and respectful if Cassandra was willing to put in the same effort.

"James has told me about your own fertility related issues," Cassandra carefully said, as if unsure she should admit she knew about Gwen's reproductive system and how much of a stubborn ass it was, like her. "I'm sorry to hear about them."

"Don't be. I'm choosing to see it as one less thing to worry about."

Gwen had said that too hastily, hadn't she? Because that was nothing but pity on Cassandra's soft face. *Shocking. The woman with a baby at her feet feels sorry for me.* "He also told me that if things go well with Patrick, he might be interested in having another child sometime in the near future."

Another lump fell into the pit of Gwen's stomach. "That's what you came over to talk about, isn't it?"

"I was under the impression it's why you invited me to drinks, yes."

"Well… jump right into it, why don't we?"

"We've passed the pleasantries. Only seems right we get to the crux of our business. I'm not sure how long Patrick will behave, anyway. I planned to stay the hour, but…"

As if on cue, Patrick propped himself up on his feet while gripping his chubby fingers around the table leg. Cassandra paused to clap for his achievement. Gwen offered him an encouraging smile.

He looked right back at her and smiled as well.

Jesus. My heart. The kid was cute. Okay, he was *adorable.* Gwen had no idea what to do with him, but James had assured her that it would get better with time. Patrick would get older, learn to talk, acquire quirks and a roaring personality, and his relationship with Gwen could be its own force to be reckoned with. But right now, when he wasn't quite yet two, Gwen only saw a vortex of the unknown. Her unknown relationship to him, her unknown relationship to her own maternal instincts, and her unknown feelings toward, well…

"It would be an excellent compromise." Gwen drank her cider as if it were water. "No worries about my own fertility problems, and I wouldn't have to go through the physical trials of motherhood, which my doctor has warned could cause me a new set of complications." Not to mention her lifelong reluctance to ever do the pregnancy and childbirth song and dance. Some women changed their minds as they grew older, but so far, Gwen was entering her thirties without a speck of change. She always assumed that, if she *really* wanted kids, she'd have to use a surrogate or adopt.

Well, if Cassandra was offering…

What better way to grab hold of the narrative by its horns and own it? Bonus points if it made the stuck-up families lose their shit in scandal.

"Obviously, it wouldn't happen soon," Gwen said. "We *all* need time to talk it over and decide what is best for *all* of us." She couldn't stress that word enough. She didn't want to be left out. She didn't want Cassandra left out, and she sure as hell couldn't forget James, who would more than likely be the father of any child the three of them came up with together.

Cassandra sipped her cider. "Of course. By the way, have you heard that Ophelia has been visiting a divorce lawyer?"

Gwen grinned. Now *there* was a topic she couldn't wait to sink her teeth into!

They gossiped for the next half hour while drinking cider and eating crackers. Patrick continued to play with his small loot of toys on the floor, but toward the end of the hour, he propped himself up again and waddled toward Gwen.

He placed a wooden car in her lap.

"Oh, *hi.*" Gwen almost choked on the cider. "What do you have?"

"That's his favorite one," Cassandra said. "We can't go anywhere unless we bring his car. This must mean he likes you!"

Gwen continued to stare at the boy plopping a toy into her lap. *What the hell do I do?* She hated to admit that she froze up whenever Patrick directly interacted with her. It was like… ah, hell, it was like she wanted to grab this boy and give him a kiss, but was afraid it would make him scream!

In time, Gwen would get better at interacting with her stepson. She would learn those crazy little quirks – such as his favorite toys, how he responded to certain events, and why she would never get away with a kiss to the top of his head – and develop her own language with a boy who would eventually come to her when he wanted to rant about his parents or ask how to ask his first crush out.

By then, he'd probably have a sibling. Maybe. Probably. Yes.

Until then, Gwen would help the boy steady his steps while handing him back his car. "Thank you!" Was that too over the top? Would this two-year-old think she was nuts? "I'll take good care of it, okay?" She pretended to hide the little car between her palms. Patrick instantly furrowed his brows and opened his mouth to protest. "Oh, you want it back? Here you go."

He slowly wrapped his fingers around the car and pulled it off her lap. The last thing he did before running back to his mother was offer her a small, coy smile that was so much like his father's that Gwen couldn't help but laugh.

Those Merange boys had a habit of stealing her heart, after all.

EPILOGUE

JAMES

James received word that the guest of honor was on her way to the ballroom. "*Five minutes,*" Charlotte Williams had texted him. "*Took some convincing after we left the spa, but we're finally heading over. You'll LOVE the dress she bought!*"

"Five minutes!" James called to the guests milling about the ballroom. Everyone was on their second glass of champagne and ready to get this party *really* started. *I can't blame them. I'm ready to* p*arty, too.* He'd be happy to start with a hard drink, but he'd wait until Gwen arrived. "Everyone get into place!"

There weren't many places to hide in a ballroom equipped for wedding receptions and surprise birthday parties. But the fifty guests, which included some of James and Gwen's closest friends and select family members, gathered in the back of the room while one of the uniformed waiters turned off most of the lights. That unfortunately included the strings of yellow party lights hanging low enough for anyone over six feet tall to bat around. James hoped some of his old frat buddies would wait until they were drunk enough to get away with it. *I chose champagne and wine for a reason, you idiots.* James needed another drink.

"Uh oh." Ian tapped his friend's shoulder when James hunkered down by one of the tables in the center of the dark ballroom. "Check it out."

He showed James his phone, currently filled with texts from Kathryn. *"I think she suspects something is up. You gentlemen better be ready for this, because Charlotte and I will try to blow smoke up James's ass so she's in a good mood when he jumps on her."*

"Jumping on her?" James scratched his head. "What does she think this is? The Dark Hour?"

"Tell me the only reason you're not having this party there is because your mom's here."

James waved to Ophelia on the other side of the room. She politely waved back before returning to her chat with another guest.

"Imagining my mom in a BDSM sex dungeon is something I can live my life without, thanks." James cleared his throat. "Sounds more like a Welsh thing, if you catch my drift."

They both looked to the *other* side of the room, where Cassandra rocked a sleeping toddler dressed in a smart little shirt and trouser set. She was the life of that half of the party, surrounded by a dozen heiresses and young trophy wives who attempted to contain their exploding ovaries.

"Say a thing about my son, and I'll clock you, Mathers." James hushed everyone after that, for he received a text from Charlotte saying they were getting out of the car.

The event coordinator hustled into the ballroom with a similar announcement. She hauled ass to the far side of the room, ensuring she wouldn't be the first thing Gwen saw when she entered the darkened room with her entourage of heiresses.

It had been an easy enough plan to concoct once he told Kathryn and Charlotte what he had in mind for Gwen's birthday. "*Take her out for a spa day and a shopping spree – I'll make sure all the reservations are made so there won't be any complications. Then tell her we're all having a birthday dinner in the restaurant at the top of the Longevity Building. She loves the gourmet burgers there, so she'll go along with it. I'll even tell her that's where I'm taking her for dinner. Instead, bring her to the ballroom.*" To make sure she didn't *really* kill him, James arranged for the restaurant to cater the party. Gwen would still get her gourmet burger for dinner.

Three feminine shadows appeared outside the door. Kathryn was the one who opened it, and Gwen followed her. "…Why are we going in *here?*" Gwen asked. "Don't tell me this is a…"

James cut her off before she could guess what had happened. While the lights popped back on and guests leaped out from behind tables screaming *Surprise!,* James flashed his wife a big, charismatic smile. Like the ones he used to seduce her into his heart and bed.

Gwen clasped her hand over her heart for one second before lowering it again, the fires of disbelief burning in her eyes. Yet that grin peppering her lips assured James that he wouldn't be castrated that night. Maybe on the morrow, but for that one night, Gwen was more than content to simply shove his shoulder and greet the guests coming up to wish her happy birthday.

"You bastard," she snapped, smirk still intact on her face. "I guessed you were up to something when these two insisted on spending an extra hour at the spa."

"What?" Charlotte's attempt at looking innocent was appreciated. "I *really* needed that extra massage. I'm soooo tight in my lower back!" She turned the moment a waiter approached them with flutes of champagne. "Ooh! Booze! 'Bout damn time!"

Everyone grabbed a fresh flute of champagne and held them up to cheer for Gwen's birthday. She abashedly muttered that she wasn't sure why everyone was making such a big deal about it. She had already turned thirty. Her current age wasn't special! They were only making such a big deal because it was a Saturday!

"They're making a big deal because you're the best, Gwenny." James took her hand and gently tapped his glass against hers. "There isn't a lady in this room who holds a candle to your beauty or matches your humility."

She rolled her eyes. "You rehearsed that, didn't you?"

James knew he couldn't say anything to change her mind, but he still stood by his declaration. *You are the most beautiful woman in the room. There's no arguing that.* Her cocktail dress was a simple light pink that hugged her knees and showed off her muscular shoulders with tiny straps that barely clung to her generous bust. Her blond hair was down and free, and her heels sensibly low to the ground. Perfect for pulling her into the small dancefloor, where James had the opportunity to put his glass down and initiate the first couple's dance of the evening. Gwen was still blushing and giggling when he kissed her and said, "Happy birthday."

"How long were you planning this for?" she asked.

He twirled her when the chorus of her favorite song played over the speakers. "Two months? Maybe three? You know me and my big plans." James pulled her back. The two of them silently swayed while other guests paired off. Laughter filled the air. Exactly what Gwen deserved on one of her many birthdays.

"I *do* know you and your big plans." Gwen gripped his shoulders and hid another smirk behind her pink lips. "Which means you have other plans as soon as we get home, yes?"

Before James could either confirm or deny such knowledge, Cassandra snuck up behind him, their son squirming in his arms. Tiny tear tracts slid down his cheeks as he momentarily reached out to his father but was inadvertently prevented from touching him. Cassandra was too flustered to do anything but rearrange her son against her chest.

"So sorry, but I think we need to head out." She patted Patrick's head. "It's getting to be his bed time, and you know how he is…"

James released one of Gwen's hands but kept the other firmly clenched. He kissed his son and cooed at him until Patrick was somewhat pacified.

"Say *bye bye*." Cassandra turned the tearful toddler to the birthday girl. "Can you say *bye bye* to Gwen?"

The sounds didn't come out, but at least Patrick made a paltry effort to mouth the words in their direction. The poor boy wanted to go to bed. *Can't blame him. He takes after me, after all. Can't be helped!* James liked his bedtime and naps, too. Patrick had a long life of wanting to do nothing but sleep half the day away before him!

"Thanks for coming to my birthday party, Patrick." Gwen placed a kind hand on his cheek. To his credit, the boy didn't shirk away from her. In fact, he reached both hands out to her, and Cassandra struggled to keep the growing toddler from falling out of her arms. "I'll make sure to come to yours soon, too!"

"I think he wants you to hold him, Gwen," James said, careful to not pressure her. "He makes that gesture when he wants to be held goodbye." It prided him to know that. He better damn well know what kind of things the kid meant with his gestures.

Gwen hesitated before opening her arms to him. Stiff arms, to be sure, but the fact she made the effort was what almost brought tears to James's eyes. Cassandra carefully passed the boy to Gwen's embrace. She stayed on standby until Gwen had her fill of bouncing the kid in her arms and saying her goodbyes. Patrick had stopped crying by the time he went to his mother.

"Have a good night." Cassandra nodded to them both with a smile before taking her leave. Gwen was the last to turn around.

"Where were we?" she asked her husband.

The birthday party was arranged to Gwen's tastes, from the food and drink to the music the DJ regaled them with. To the eternal sounds of The Cranberries, James continued to twirl his wife across the dancefloor and occasionally fielded cheeky questions from the guests who knew nothing about their relationship. Forever a secret except to a select few.

Until tonight.

James stopped dancing at the end of "Dreams" and held Gwen out at arm's length. He fished into his pocket while the DJ cut the next song and everyone in the small ballroom turned toward them.

Gwen looked around as if she were about to be pranked.

"Gwenyth Mitchell," James said, sweat dripping from his fingers and into her palm. "You are the most wonderful woman I have met in my life. Who knew that me stumbling into a random bar one night would bring my soulmate into my life?"

"That's fate, bro!" an old frat brother yelled over the heads of the crowd. People chuckled. Gwen blushed.

"I think it's a crime that the whole world doesn't know what we really mean to each other." When he got down on one knee and pulled out the ring they picked out for their elopement two years ago, Gwen nearly passed out. "Do me the honors of publicly being my wife, would you?"

Chuckles turned into awe. At first, James worried that he had committed a great faux pas against his wife. Not like he had run this by her first!

Gwen unleashed the most conniving smile he had ever seen grace her beautiful face. "Why, James," she said with fake candor, "are you asking me to *finally* marry you? On my birthday? Oh, dreams come true!"

He picked up her cue and ran with it. "Yup! Gonna marry you on your birthday! How does next year sound?"

"Plenty of time to dump all your cash into the wedding of the year!"

James looked to his friends, who shrugged, then to his mother, who also shrugged. Nobody would save his ass tonight. "You want a wedding, huh?"

Gwen crossed her arms and *shrugged.* The tables had turned on James Merange, and he had nobody to blame but himself. "I want the world, James. We can start with a fancy little wedding. Now, come give me a big engagement kiss."

Only a few people in the ballroom knew what was so funny about this situation. Honestly, it was the perfect prank for James to play on everyone, from his mother, to his best friends, to the woman now in his arms and sharing a kiss with him. Raucous applause erupted. The only sound they heard between the beating of their hearts, however, was Charlotte sneaking up to them and whispering, "If I'm not the maid of honor, you're dead to me," into Gwen's ear.

"She… doesn't know we're already married, right?" Gwen asked as soon as Charlotte disappeared back into the crowd.

"I never told her."

Gwen shook her head. "The girl ain't right."

James squeezed her closer to his body. Her arms flung around his shoulders, and their noses lightly rubbed together. James could have kissed her again. Instead, he said, "Good thing you're the right one for me."

They kissed to more applause. Gwen flexed her finger boasting her wedding ring against the back of her husband's neck and whispered the naughty things she wanted to do with him that night. Funny. He already had *all* of that planned. *It's almost like we're on the same wavelength or something!*

As soon as the music began again, he dipped her over his arm and looked deep into her eyes. He saw nothing but love… and the same curious expression she gave him that first night he walked into her bar.

If she never lost that look in her eyes, then James would know that they were destined for an eternity of bliss – probably with no dull moments.

Cynthia Dane spends most of her time writing in the great Pacific Northwest. And when she's not writing, she's dreaming up her next big plot and meeting all sorts of new characters in her head.

She loves stories that are sexy, fun, and cut right to the chase. You can always count on explosive romances - both in and out of the bedroom - when you read a Cynthia Dane story.

Falling in love. Making love. Love in all shades and shapes and sizes. Cynthia loves it all!

Connect with Cynthia on any of the following:

Website: http://www.cynthiadane.com
Twitter: http://twitter.com/cynthia_dane
Facebook: http://facebook.com/authorcynthiadane

Printed in Great Britain
by Amazon

36980565R00118